Notes from the desk of Amanda Blake

It's been more than a month since Eli Coulter has allowed me access to his mother's journals. Melanie Coulter was an amazing, talented woman, and I'm learning more about her every day. Eli, however, remains a mystery. Why won't he trust me? And why is it so important to me that he does? He has made it abundantly clear that he doesn't want me around. But I know I can't be the only one who feels the sparks between us....

Dear Reader,

My parents nurtured and encouraged my love of writing and reading, so it's no surprise to me that I grew up to become an author. But what would have happened if they had not? I've always wondered how I would have coped, and in Eli's story, I had a chance to explore some possible alternatives.

A gifted artist like his mother, Eli Coulter had to deal with his widowed father's attempts to ban art from Eli's life. Despite the overwhelming obstacles, Eli succeeded by limiting his deeper emotional connections and focusing fiercely on his work. But when his father dies and Eli is called home to the Montana ranch where he grew up, he meets a beautiful reporter named Amanda Blake. It isn't long before he realizes happiness requires more than fulfilling work—he needs Amanda.

I hope you enjoy Eli and Amanda's story and that you'll return with me soon to the Triple C Ranch for Brodie Coulter's story.

Best,

~Lois

A COULTER'S CHRISTMAS PROPOSAL

LOIS FAYE DYER

Harlequin

SPECIAL EDITION

Recycling programs
for this product may
not exist in your area.

ISBN-13: 978-0-373-65634-9

A COULTER'S CHRISTMAS PROPOSAL

Books by Lois Faye Dyer

Harlequin Special Edition

‡*The Virgin and Zach Coulter* #2116
‡*A Coulter's Christmas Proposal* #2152

Silhouette Special Edition

He's Got His Daddy's Eyes #1129
The Cowboy Takes a Wife #1198
The Only Cowboy for Caitlin #1253
Cattleman's Courtship #1306
Cattleman's Bride-to-Be #1457
Practice Makes Pregnant #1569
Cattleman's Heart #1605
The Prince's Bride #1640
Luke's Proposal #1745
Jesse's Child #1776
Chase's Promise #1791
Trey's Secret #1823
**The Princess and the Cowboy* #1865
†*Triple Trouble* #1957
Quinn McCloud's Christmas Bride #2007
††*Cinderella and the Playboy* #2036
‡*Cade Coulter's Return* #2074
**Beauty and the Wolf* #2091

*The McClouds of Montana
**The Hunt for Cinderella
†Fortunes of Texas: Return to Red Rock
††The Baby Chase
‡Big Sky Brothers

LOIS FAYE DYER

lives in a small town on the shore of beautiful Puget Sound in the Pacific Northwest with her two eccentric and lovable cats, Chloe and Evie. She loves to hear from readers. You can write to her c/o Paperbacks Plus, 1618 Bay Street, Port Orchard, WA 98366. Visit her on the web at www.LoisDyer.com.

Huge thanks to the Tuesday Morning Breakfast Club—
you keep me sane...

Prologue

Mid-July
San Luis, Spain

The hot Spanish sunshine poured over the little town square of San Luis. Eli Coulter left the relative comfort of a shaded seat, weaving his way around diners breakfasting at other umbrella-topped tables clustered outside the café doorway. His mind reeled as he processed the information an American investigator had relayed only moments earlier.

Zach and Cade are back on the Triple C. Does that mean something happened to Dad? Even if Joseph was dead, Eli couldn't help but wonder why his brothers were at the ranch. There was no possibility their father had left them anything in his will.

Joseph Coulter hated all four of his sons with equal animosity.

Eli strode swiftly up the cobblestone street to the sprawling stucco home of his host, reclusive sculptor Lucan Montoya. For the past year, the elderly Spaniard had been Eli's mentor. The apprenticeship had proven invaluable; only two weeks remained of their time together and Eli was reluctant to see it end.

He'd considered staying on in San Luis once his apprenticeship had ended. But if his brothers needed him, that changed everything.

Given the remoteness of the small Spanish village and its lack of cell phone service, it took nearly an hour to reach his brother Zach.

"What?"

Eli grinned at Zach's impatient demand. "The least you could do is say 'hello, how are you?'" he commented mildly.

"Eli?" Zach's deep voice held surprise and relief. "Damn, it's about time you called. Where are you?"

"I'm in Spain," Eli told him. "I've been here for months. I've been meaning to check in but my cell phone doesn't get service here. A detective showed up today and told me I needed to call you."

"We've been looking for you, Eli." Zach's voice turned grim. "The old man died."

Eli hadn't seen his father in thirteen years but hearing Zach confirm what he'd suspected had the power to stun him. Shock held him silent.

"Dad left the Triple C and nearly everything else he owned to the four of us," Zach went on.

"That's impossible," Eli said flatly, finding his voice. "He hated our guts. Why would he leave us the ranch?"

"Apparently he sobered up and had a change of heart after we left," Zach told him.

"I'll be damned." Eli didn't know what to make of the news. "I never thought he'd stop drinking—or stop hating us."

"Me either," Zach admitted.

"So." Eli tried to focus on the here and now, and not on the memories pushing to get out of the box he'd locked them in years ago. "When did he die?"

"Last December. It took the attorney several months to find Cade, and then he found me through my office. Cade's running the ranch and I've almost got the Lodge ready to open again. Dad left the Triple C to all four of us but he left specific pieces to each of us. He left you Mom's studio, Eli."

Again, Eli was stunned into silence. Melanie Coulter had been a sculptor on the brink of becoming world-famous when a tragic accident while swimming with her four sons in the creek near her studio had taken her life. The day of her funeral, Joseph Coulter had sealed her studio and forbidden his sons to enter.

"The inheritance taxes on the ranch are huge and there aren't any cash assets. We need you to come home," Zach continued. "The only way we're going to save the place is if we all stick together and find a way to make this work."

"I'll come," Eli said slowly, shaking off the shock that held him and considering the logistics. "I have two more weeks here to finalize a commission but maybe I can complete it faster." He frowned, thinking with lightning speed. "Where's Brodie?" he asked. "Is he there with you?"

Zach's slight pause filled Eli with foreboding.

"He's in California," Zach said finally.

"Why isn't he with you and Cade at the ranch?"

"He was hurt, got thrown by a bull and shattered his leg." Zach's voice was serious. "He's done riding rodeo."

"Damn," Eli muttered. He'd talked to Brodie just before he'd left for Spain and his brother had been fine. Brodie was a year older than him, and rodeo had been his life since he was old enough to climb on a horse. He had been named all-around champion three times and, after years of hard work, was at the top of his career. Eli couldn't imagine a life for Brodie that didn't include rodeo.

"Cade and I went to see him.... He's in a hospital recovery center in Ukiah, north of San Francisco."

"Is he coming to the ranch when they release him?"

"He said he wouldn't, but Cade and I hope he will."

Eli drew in a deep breath and exhaled slowly. "All right. Have you got a pen? Here's my landline phone number if you need to reach me." Eli quickly recited Lucan's number. "If you don't hear from me again, don't worry. I'm going to be working flat out to finish here. Then I'll head back to Montana."

"Great. I'll tell Cade. And, Eli..."

"Yeah?"

"I'm glad you're coming home." Zach's voice rasped, roughened with feeling.

"See you soon." Eli had mixed feelings. He'd be glad to see his brothers. But returning to the Triple C and all the bad memories the ranch would surely hold?

He wasn't at all sure he was looking forward to that part of the trip.

Chapter One

August
Montana

Two weeks later the jet airplane carrying Eli began its descent in preparation for landing in Billings.

He yawned, scrubbed his hand over his face and rubbed his eyes. He'd left Spain nearly three days ago, and the long drive from San Luis to Madrid, followed by an endless round of waiting in airports and hours spent sitting on planes, had left his eyes feeling gritty, burning from lack of sleep.

He blinked to clear his vision and gazed out the window. Far below, the distinctive rise of tall buttes stood out amid rolling miles of sage prairie that stretched from horizon to horizon.

I should be at the Triple C in another four hours, give or take, he thought. He'd rent a vehicle to drive the last three hours north from Billings to reach Indian Springs. There were no planes, trains or buses that could take him on the last stage of his journey home to rural Montana.

And that was one of the things he'd always loved about the Triple C. Homesteaded by his Coulter ancestors in the late eighteen hundreds, the huge ranch sprawled over thousands of acres. Eli remembered his mother telling him the Triple C was one of the biggest spreads in Montana, second only to the slightly larger McCloud Ranch to the north.

He still had trouble believing the Triple C now belonged to him and his brothers. Thirteen years ago, driving away from the land he loved had been gut-wrenching. Nevertheless, he'd been determined to leave the chaos of life with his alcoholic father and his increasingly frequent explosions of rage and violence.

He'd wanted peace and the ability to control his own destiny. Most of all, he'd wanted the freedom to focus on becoming a better artist. He'd traveled the world since then, never putting down roots, and, over time, he'd convinced himself he no longer missed Montana and the sprawling Triple C.

But with the landscape of prairie spread out below him, beneath Montana's cloudless blue sky, he had to wonder if he'd been kidding himself.

The pilot's voice sounded in the cabin, pulling Eli's brooding gaze and attention away from the view outside his window.

An hour later he had landed, rented a pickup truck, and was driving north on the highway toward Indian Springs. Neither Cade nor Zach had answered their phones when he'd called to tell them he'd landed, so he'd left messages saying he was on his way home. He wasn't surprised when they didn't return his calls. During summer, ranchers worked long hours and were often out of range of cell reception. He figured he'd reach the ranch before they even got his messages.

The late-afternoon sun slanted into the cab, heating the interior. Eli left the window rolled down, his arm resting on the sill, the breeze filling the cab with the scent of sage and clean, clear air unclogged by smog and exhaust.

The digital clock on the dashboard told him it was just after 9:00 p.m. when he slowed, turning off the highway to drive beneath a high arch of wrought iron that spelled out Coulter Cattle Company. The formal name had long ago been shortened to the Triple C by family and locals.

The gravel ranch road was smooth beneath the truck's wheels. Eli's lips curved in a faint smile.

I can tell Cade's home, he thought. His oldest brother's attention to detail was thorough and Cade had never put up with potholes for long. Each of the boys had become adept at using the blade on the big John Deere tractor to grade the gravel road and keep it in good condition. But Cade had been the best at moving snow in winter and smoothing out ridges in spring and summer.

Eli crested a rise and he caught his first look at his childhood home. Across the valley below him, beyond the creek and its bridge, was the cluster of buildings that made up the headquarters of the Triple C.

Something soothed, settled inside Eli. Surprised, he absentmindedly rubbed his hand over the left side of his chest.

What the hell? He hadn't expected to feel anything good. He hadn't wanted to come back to Montana, and if Zach hadn't told him he was needed, he would have gone back to New Mexico when he left Spain.

Lights winked on in the cluster of buildings across the valley and Eli realized that full dark wasn't far away. Northeast Montana wasn't quite far enough north to share Alaska's midnight sun, but during the summer months, sunset was much later than he'd grown accustomed to in southern Spain. He remembered being a boy and spending summer evenings playing baseball outside until long after 9:00 p.m., before darkness finally prevented him and his brothers from seeing the ball.

He took his foot off the brake, the truck picking up speed as he drove across the valley and rattled over the bridge before reaching the house and outbuildings. The muted sound of music floated in the open cab windows as he switched off the engine and pushed open the door.

Eli paused as the music struck a chord with him. What was it Zach had said when Eli called to tell him he was on his way home?

Oh, yeah, he thought. *Zach said he's having a party to reopen the Lodge.*

He frowned, trying to calculate days and failing. He didn't remember what day it was exactly but figured there was a good chance the Lodge opening was tonight.

He glanced at the house, dark except for the glowing light over the door on the front porch.

His stomach chose that moment to rumble in loud protest.

If Zach's throwing a party, there has to be food, he thought.

Eli pulled the pickup door closed again and switched on the engine once more, leaving the ranch yard to drive down the gravel lane that led from the house and barns and along the creek to the Lodge.

He rounded a bend, and before him the Lodge and its grounds were ablaze with light. Couples strolled across the drive and onto the lawn that slanted down to the creek.

Eli eased the truck around the circular drive, stopping to let guests pass in front of his bumper, and double-parked in front of the main entryway.

Without giving a thought to his faded jeans, boots and travel-wrinkled shirt, he stepped out onto the drive and climbed the shallow steps to the long porch that nearly circled the Lodge.

He stepped inside the lobby and halted, his gaze searching the crowd for Cade and Zach.

Amanda Blake sipped champagne, the crystal flute cool in her hand, and tried to pay attention to the conversation. She stood with her friends, a married couple who were the delighted winners of opening-week reservations at the Lodge, and two other couples. Despite the interesting company, however, her focus wandered as she looked about the beautiful lobby of the Coulter Lodge. The expansive area was thronged with guests. Men in suits and women in cocktail dresses mingled with ranchers wearing pearl-snapped Western shirts, bolo ties and cowboy boots. Scattered through the crowd were several girls in pretty summer dresses casting glances at teenage boys in crisp shirts, slacks and boots.

Clearly, she thought with approval, the Coulters had

invited not only their guests and out-of-town media people, but also their neighbors and local friends, creating a vibrant mix. The high-ceilinged room was filled with chatter and laughter that occasionally drowned out the four musicians stationed at the far end of the room.

She half turned from her small group, letting her gaze skim the room, taking in the huge stone fireplace at one end, the massive silver-and-copper sculpture of mustangs in full gallop mounted on the wall behind the reception desk. Amusement curved her mouth as she noted a small cluster of teenagers giggling in the corner before she shifted her attention to the main entry.

Amanda made a mental note to thank her friends for inviting her tonight. This inside view of the newly renovated Coulter Lodge provided invaluable information for the biography she was writing on Melanie Coulter, the artist who had created the fabulous wall sculpture of horses.

And if she was lucky, she thought, perhaps she would have another chance to speak to the artist's sons Cade and Zach Coulter about granting her an interview. They hadn't been cooperative when she'd approached them nearly a week ago, but she hadn't given up hope of finding a way to convince them.

She narrowed her eyes, wondering idly how tall the custom entry door was since the carved piece over the top seemed much higher than normal.

Her musings were abruptly interrupted by the man who stepped over the threshold and into the room, halting a few feet inside.

Amanda caught her breath, feeling her eyes go wide as she stared.

He was dressed in a rumpled white shirt, open at the

neck, the sleeves rolled back over powerful forearms. Faded jeans covered his long legs and he wore dusty black cowboy boots.

His attire was far more casual than any of the other guests' but it wasn't his clothing that riveted Amanda. He had coal-black hair that fell from a widow's peak to brush against the collar of his shirt at his nape. The planes of his face were sharp and clear, with high, sculpted cheekbones and a strong jaw, his mouth sensual below a straight nose. But it was the eyes that held her the most. Below slashes of eyebrows as black as the glossy fall of his shaggy hair, his thick-lashed eyes were astonishingly, unbelievably green—so pale a green they seemed overlaid with ice.

Amanda shivered. He exuded an aura of quiet, restrained power that seemed to vibrate the very air around him. He appeared supremely unconcerned that guests were turning to look at him as his gaze moved over the room.

As she watched, unable to look away, the stranger's mouth curved, a smile lighting his face, turning it from handsome to movie-star gorgeous.

Cade and Zach Coulter strode through the crowd and reached him, taking turns to clasp his hand and pull him into hard hugs.

With the three black-haired, green-eyed, tall and powerful men standing side by side, recognition hit Amanda like a freight train.

Oh, my God. That's Eli Coulter.

"Damn, Eli," Cade said, his eyes warm, his deep voice raspy with emotion. "What's with the hair? You couldn't find a barber in Spain?"

"Not one I wanted to let near me with sharp scissors," Eli told him with a grin.

"We let you out of our sight for a year and you come home looking like a girl," Zach told him with an affectionate smile.

"Yeah, right," Eli said dryly. Like both Cade and Zach, Eli knew his voice was unsteady, the tones rougher than usual. With silent acceptance, he recognized and acknowledged the deep undercurrent of emotion that lay beneath their teasing. He always enjoyed catching up with his brothers whenever they managed to get together. But this time, their reunion held deeper, more powerful implications. Joseph Coulter's death had shifted the playing field, and despite his long estrangement from his father, Eli knew Joseph's passing had changed what he'd come to accept as normal. They'd all have to come to terms with a future that had a vastly different landscape. He jerked his chin at the brightly lit, crowded lobby. "Quite a party you're throwing."

"Yup." Zach turned, his gaze moving over the huge room. "We invited all the Lodge guests, plus all the neighbors and everyone in town who wanted to come. You know Indian Springs. Folks can't turn down an invitation to a party."

Eli grinned. "I remember." His smile faded as he scanned the room. "You've done a great job with the place, Zach. Looks just like I remembered it."

"I wanted it restored to the original plan," Zach said as Cade turned, too, and both of their gazes followed Eli's to take in the crowded lobby. "The furniture is different, of course, but the rest of the building is pretty much like it was."

"Except for the kitchen," a feminine voice put in. "It's been updated and is way more efficient."

Eli looked over his shoulder to find two women, both blondes. Zach draped his arm around the shoulders of the woman who'd spoken, pulled her close and dropped a kiss on her temple as she leaned into him. She was gorgeous, her lush female curves highlighted in a short, red silk dress. And she clearly belonged to Zach, Eli thought, noting the possessive way his brother held her tucked against his side.

"Eli, I'd like you to meet Cynthia," Zach said, "my fiancée."

Eli felt his eyes widen. He looked from Zach's face to the beautiful woman, noting the ease with which she accepted his brother's touch. "Well, I'll be damned," he said softly. "I never thought I'd see the day a woman was brave enough to take you on." He held out his hand. "Nice to meet you, Cynthia."

She slipped her small, soft hand into his and gave him a warm smile.

Before she could respond, Cade broke in.

"And this is Mariah," he said, "*my* fiancée."

Stunned, Eli swung his attention to his oldest brother and found that the other striking blonde now had her arm tucked through the bend of Cade's elbow. She wore a deep blue dress that made her long sheaf of pale hair look like ripe wheat. Her brown eyes sparkled with amusement as her gaze met his.

"You too?" He shook his head slowly. "Damn, is there something in the water here I need to look out for?"

Both Mariah and Cynthia laughed.

"I don't think it's the water, Eli, but you might want to be careful around pretty blondes," Cade said wryly.

"Yeah, I'll do that." He took Mariah's hand, just as small, just as soft as Cynthia's had been, in his much larger one. "Nice to meet you, too, Mariah."

"It's lovely to see you here at last, Eli," Mariah said, her voice warm. "I'm looking forward to getting to know all of Cade's brothers."

"I wish we didn't have to play host at this party," Cade told him. "We've got a lot to talk about."

"Yeah," Eli agreed. "But it can keep. Truth is, I'm starving." He nodded at the long buffet table against the far wall. "While you're circulating and charming the guests, I'll get some food and find a quiet place to sit down."

"Don't miss the miniature chocolate cakes with fudge icing," Cynthia told him. "They're fabulous."

"Or the little pumpkin tarts," Mariah added.

"Fill a plate at the table with whatever looks good. Then head down the hall to the kitchen," Zach told him. "The chef's name is Jane, and if you want something more substantial than the buffet food, just ask her."

"As soon as this breaks up, we'll join you in the kitchen," Cade said.

"Sounds good." Eli nodded and turned to make his way to the buffet table while the other four mingled with the crowd.

He couldn't believe his brothers were getting married. Marriage wasn't even on his radar screen—not even a remote possibility. He couldn't imagine himself falling in love, risking his heart, perhaps his sanity, maybe even his life, if the marriage didn't work out. His own parents' marriage had seemed idyllic to his youthful eyes. But after his mother's death, when Eli was nine years old, his father had been unable to function without his wife and had proceeded to drown himself in alcohol and rage. Life had become a nightmare and Eli couldn't imagine himself signing on for any part of the commitment and potential heartbreak of marriage.

As an adult, after watching his friends marry and divorce over the years, he'd decided marriages had a lousy success rate.

Still, given the way Cade and Zach had looked at their women, and Mariah and Cynthia had looked back at them, Eli had a feeling his brothers had a better than average chance to beat the odds.

He took a plate and worked his way down the length of the white-cloth-covered buffet table. If the food tasted even half as good as it looked and smelled, he thought, Zach had found a chef worth keeping. He reached the end of the table and turned away, realizing too late he'd stepped back into someone.

"Sorry, I..." He glanced over his shoulder and paused, then pivoted fully to look down at the woman. "My apologies," he said, flicking a quick, intent look over the female curves encased in a slim black cocktail dress.

Petite and curvy, she had world-class legs, with trim ankles and small feet tucked into black strappy shoes with impossibly high heels. The hem of the dress ended just above her knees, and the black material looked soft as silk, clinging to the curves of thighs, hips, narrow waist and full breasts. Her thick brown hair was streaked with paler gold and fell to her shoulders in a sleek curve. Behind the thin black frame of narrow eyeglasses that perched on the bridge of her small, straight nose, her eyes were hazel. Those thick-lashed eyes widened as she looked up at him, and the soft pink bow of her mouth parted in surprise.

Eli instantly wondered just how soft her lips were and realized with a start of surprise that it had been a long time since any woman had interested him this much, this fast.

Amanda jolted when someone bumped into her, and she quickly held her flute away from her dress as the champagne sloshed toward the rim. She turned, words of annoyance freezing in her throat as she looked up into pale green eyes. Eyes that heated as Eli's gaze swept her from head to toe, returning to her face while he granted her an incredibly attractive, very male smile.

"Are you all right?" he asked.

Amanda realized she'd been silent, staring up at him in fascination, and felt her cheeks heat as she flushed. "I'm fine," she said quickly.

"I didn't make you spill that, did I?" He gestured at the flute in her hand.

"No, not at all." She looked back at him. "You don't have a glass. Don't you like champagne?"

"I prefer whiskey but champagne works, too," he said with a drawl, his eyes inviting her to smile with him.

And smile she did, helpless to deny the charm of that smile and the focused, heated intensity in his eyes.

"Have you eaten yet?" he asked.

"No, I…"

"Good. Then you can join me. I hate eating alone," he said smoothly. He lifted a plate from the stack nearest them and handed it to her, then settled his hand at her waist and turned her toward the table. "I have it on good authority that the little pumpkin pie things are good," he told her.

"Tarts," she said automatically.

"What?" He looked bemused.

"The pumpkin pie things—they're tarts."

"Oh, yeah. Tarts." He smiled at her.

She smiled back, knowing she was asking for trouble. She should tell him her name and why she was visiting Indian Springs. He clearly didn't know who she was, and the minute he found out, he'd stop smiling and tell her to leave. His brothers had been polite when she'd approached them to ask for their cooperation with the biography about their mother. But they'd firmly refused, then hustled her out of their offices and off the Triple C.

She didn't doubt Eli would do the same.

But she didn't want him to stop looking at her with that interested male awareness that made her shiver. Not yet. So she allowed him to pile food on her plate as they moved along the laden table.

When her plate was full, Eli cupped her elbow and guided her to an alcove that held a small table and two chairs. The intimate seating was out of the flow of traffic and semiprivate.

"I just realized," he said as he held her chair before dropping into the other seat to join her, "you haven't told me your name."

Her heart sank.

"It's Amanda…Amanda Blake."

"And what are you doing here tonight, Amanda Blake?" he asked. "Are you a guest at the Lodge?"

His eyebrows lifted in query, his even white teeth biting into one of the tarts he'd insisted she try, as well.

"No, I'm not," she told him. "I'm staying at the hotel in Indian Springs."

"So you're not a local girl. Let me guess...." His eyes narrowed, studying her. "New York?"

She felt her eyes widen, again. Apparently, Eli Coulter had an endless ability to surprise her.

"You're right. I live in New York. How did you know?"

"You couldn't have found that dress and those shoes in Indian Springs, and it's not casual enough for L.A. Plus, you've got a slight East Coast accent." He smiled, his eyes curious. "New York's a long way from Indian Springs. What are you doing here in Montana?"

Oh, how she wished he hadn't asked that. Amanda lowered her fork, took a fortifying sip of champagne and smoothed her fingers over the snowy-white napkin spread over her lap.

"I'm doing research for a book I'm writing."

"Really? What kind of book? Fiction or nonfiction?"

"It's a biography, actually."

His green eyes sharpened, alert as he studied her. "And the subject of the biography is...?"

"Melanie Coulter."

His eyes flared with swift surprise, followed just as quickly by a darker flash of anger, before shutters slammed down, his face suddenly remote. "My mother," he said flatly. "You're writing a book about my mother."

"Yes," she said, mourning the loss of his warmth. He was still focused on her, but now the male interest was absent. He studied her with as much detachment as if she were a fly on the end of a pin, ready for a biology class experiment. "I've spoken with your brothers. I'd like to interview all of you."

"No." There was no emotion in the word. Just a flat rejection.

Disappointed, Amanda stiffened her spine and continued. "If you want the world to know the truth about your mother and the history of her art, you can be assured that will happen if you agree to help me tell her story."

"No." He shoved back his chair and stood. "I'm sure I speak for all my brothers when I tell you that's never going to happen. Go back to New York. There isn't a story here."

"But there is," she said earnestly, rising to face him. "Your mother has become an icon in the art world. The story of her life is going to be told, either by me or someone else. If you allow me to interview you for my project, I promise I'll not print anything you tell me in confidence. At least you'll have some measure of control over how your mother's story is presented to the world."

"The world will just have to go on believing whatever the hell they want to believe." His deep voice was grim, underlaid with a rumble of anger. "It's what they've always done."

He turned and stalked off.

What did he mean by that? The cryptic comment set off her investigative instincts. Frustrated, Amanda could only watch his broad-shouldered, powerful figure cleave through the crowd until he disappeared down a hallway. Clearly, there were deeper issues he hadn't been willing to explain.

Still, she wasn't sure if she was more disappointed

that he'd refused to help with her research or if she mourned the loss of that focused, heated male attention as he'd stared at her and smiled.

Amanda lifted her flute and sipped, but she could hardly swallow past the lump of disappointment in her throat.

She was very much afraid it was the loss of his interest in her that grieved her most.

Chapter Two

Eli entered the kitchen and paused, realizing his anger had carried him out of the lobby, down the hall and through the doorway without conscious thought.

Damn, he thought with frustration. He'd known returning to the Triple C wouldn't be easy but he hadn't expected trouble to come from a pretty stranger. He'd been back on the ranch for less than an hour.

She'd caught him off guard. He hadn't felt such an instant, powerful attraction to a woman in months. He frowned, considering…. Maybe it was longer than months. Maybe it was years.

Just his luck, she was writing a book about his mother.

No way in hell did he want somebody poking into life on the Triple C after his mother died. That bad chunk of time was better left forgotten.

But if she dug around, asked questions, she was certain to find out more than he wanted her to know about Joseph Coulter and his sons. And what she didn't piece together from what folks told her, she could probably guess.

And wouldn't that make sensational fodder for selling a book? Eli rubbed his eyes and bit off a curse, weary from more than the long journey from Spain to Montana. He lowered his hand and frowned blackly at the gleaming tiled island centered in the big room.

"Can I help you with something, Mr. Coulter?"

The clear, polite female question brought his head up.

A woman stood at the stove, her slender body wrapped in a white chef's jacket and black slacks. Dark blue embroidered letters on the jacket's pocket spelled out J. Howard. Her fair skin, reddish-blond hair and slim curves added up to a very attractive package, but he realized with annoyance that he was still too focused on Amanda Blake to care.

"You're the chef," Eli said. It wasn't a question. He inhaled deeply and nearly groaned aloud when the rich aromas of grilled beef and subtle spices filled his senses.

"Yes, I am." Her level gaze assessed him. "And you must be Zach's brother Eli. We heard you were expected. If you didn't see anything on the buffet table that appealed to you, I'm happy to prepare something else."

"I don't want to put you to any trouble," Eli said. The words had barely left his mouth before his stomach growled—loudly.

The chef smiled. "It's no trouble at all. And I can

recommend the steaks. They're from Triple C's own beef."

"I think I'd kill for a steak," Eli said fervently.

Jane shot him a sympathetic glance. "Baked potato? Salad?"

"Yes to both."

Eli crossed to the deep sink to wash up. By the time he'd dried his hands and taken a seat at the island, the steak was sizzling and filling the air with a tantalizing aroma. His stomach rumbled in anticipation.

While he waited for his meal, he brooded over his conversation with Amanda. He didn't want a reporter digging into his mother's life. He was convinced Amanda would inevitably ask questions about what happened to Melanie's family after her sudden death. Neither he nor his brothers wanted the story of their father's alcoholic rages and the unraveling of their childhood exposed in a book. His gut told him it would be like ripping open a barely healed wound when the inevitable publicity meant they'd all have to revisit bad memories. Life after their mother died had been a nightmare. He'd prefer to never again have to think about those years.

And if Amanda Blake was hell bent on conducting research for the story of his mother's life, she'd stir up all the old stories in Indian Springs.

Too bad she can't just focus her work on the good days prior to Mom's accident, he thought morosely as he watched the chef remove a thick steak from the grill.

"I appreciate this," he told Jane when she slid a plate onto the counter in front of him a moment later.

"Not a problem," she assured him. The door to the hallway pushed inward and crowd noise from the lobby was suddenly much louder. "Just stay out of the way of the servers," she warned him with a smile as three women and two men hurried in, carrying empty trays.

Eli ignored their curious glances and focused on the food. Two of the servers left with loaded trays, and by the time another two exited, the first two had returned with more empty trays.

When Eli finished eating, he carried his plate and utensils to the sink, rinsed and stacked them, and waited to catch Jane's eye to nod his thanks before leaving the room. He paused in the hallway, considering for a moment whether to return to the lobby. Did he want to avoid Amanda—or was he hoping to run into her again? He frowned, wondering why it mattered, before he pushed the question aside. He was too tired to figure out the answer. Instead of returning to the lobby, where the decrease in the level of noise told him the party must be winding down, he turned right down the hallway and entered the office.

Just as he'd hoped, a leather sofa stood along one wall, and he stretched out on the cushions, crossing his booted feet at the ankle. But each time he closed his eyes, the image of Amanda Blake's hazel eyes and lush pink lips, parted in surprise as she'd turned to look up at him, flashed in vivid color on the inside of his eyelids.

Exhausted, he managed to doze fitfully as the sounds of the party became gradually muted outside the closed door.

With Eli's departure, Amanda no longer found the Lodge so intriguing and she located her friends, said good-night and left the crowded lobby.

As she drove back to Indian Springs and parked outside her old-fashioned, two-story hotel, the memory of those moments spent talking with Eli Coulter dominated her thoughts. The instant he'd learned she was researching his mother's life story, his green eyes had cooled, his expression suddenly remote.

His reaction matched that of his brothers Cade and Zach when she'd approached them with a request for an interview.

And look how well that ended, she thought wryly as she climbed the stairway and entered her quiet hotel room.

Apparently, none of the Coulters were willing to discuss their mother.

Sighing, Amanda stripped off her clothes, hanging her little black dress in the closet and tucking underwear and hose neatly into a laundry bag before turning on the shower.

Twenty minutes later, her face scrubbed free of makeup, the ends of her hair damp, she folded back the sheets, propped fat pillows against the headboard and settled into bed with her laptop and a mug of hot green tea.

She opened the file with notes on Melanie Coulter and spent several moments jotting down her impressions of the Lodge.

Try as she might, she couldn't seem to stay focused on details of the Lodge. As she paused to sip her tea, her thoughts once again drifted to Eli. The brothers looked very much alike with their black hair, green eyes, powerful bodies and frames over six feet tall. All of them were unquestionably handsome and aggressively male.

But only Eli had made her pulse pound and her heart race.

The intense physical reaction she'd felt had surprised her. She'd never felt anything quite like it before. Even now, with time and distance separating her from him, her pulse beat slightly faster at the thought of him.

She'd met good-looking, charming men before, but there was something unique about the alert intelligence in Eli's green eyes and the way he seemed to listen intently when she spoke, as if she were the only person in the room. He'd had an easy, unforced patience while he waited for her to choose as they'd filled their plates at the buffet table. In fact, everything about him had intrigued her and made her want to learn more about the man behind the handsome face and sexy body.

Clearly, however, nothing would come of her interest, since he'd obviously put her on the don't-speak-to list.

She sighed, considering her options. She had four months left of a six-month leave of absence from her job as an editor and occasional reporter for the *Artist*, a glossy monthly periodical with offices in New York City. She'd spent the first two months researching Melanie Coulter's art. It wasn't necessary to leave her Village apartment in New York for the early research since many of the people she'd wanted to interview—Melanie's one-time agent, the art gallery that had sponsored her first showing and prominent collectors of her work—lived either in the city or within driving distance.

Her trip to Montana was the first away-from-home research she'd done for the book. She'd keenly anticipated doing on-site interviews with the people who'd been a part of Melanie Coulter's everyday life.

But while the residents of Indian Springs had been friendly and polite, they'd been surprisingly vague about details when it came to the Coulter family. And the brothers themselves had been downright uncooperative.

Amanda unconsciously tapped her fingertips against her thigh and frowned. She was tempted to think there was a local conspiracy to withhold any information about Melanie Coulter. Melanie was a well-known figure and, by the very nature of her work, had achieved a certain level of fame. While her name wasn't a household word everywhere in America, she certainly was well-known in art circles.

Puzzled by the mystery, Amanda searched the internet, clicking on several sites, only to stop at a website she'd been to before. The Fordham Gallery in San Francisco had artist photos of their regular contributors and she clicked on the page that featured Eli Coulter. He wore a Stetson, the brim of the cowboy hat pulled low over his brow in a pose that did more to conceal than reveal. The head shot was clearly professionally done and Amanda guessed the photographer had purposely found a way to create a sexy yet mysterious photo.

She scanned the brief note below that told fans there were no exhibits currently scheduled for Eli but the Gallery hoped to hold one sometime during the following year.

Quickly clicking through the information pages, she noticed there hadn't been an exhibit in more than a year.

She wondered where he'd been and what he'd been doing that resulted in his falling off the gallery's list for such a long time. Could there have been a woman involved? This random thought filled her with inexplicable jealousy.

Despite spending the next hour searching the internet and browsing websites for information, Amanda didn't find anything that would explain why any of the Coulters were so reluctant to talk with her about their mother.

She turned off her laptop, shifting it to rest on the nightstand before she snapped off the lamp and pushed all but one of the pillows to the far side of the bed. Lying flat, she tucked the sheet and blanket under her arms and stared up at the ceiling.

I have to find a way to get people to talk to me and share their memories of Melanie Coulter, she thought. The concept for her book relied on personal touches. She wanted to tell readers not only about Melanie's artistic successes but also about the woman behind the unique artwork.

Eli's eyes are like hers, she mused. Despite her need to find a way to break through the reserve of Indian Springs' residents and get them to confide in her, she couldn't keep her thoughts from returning to Eli.

She was surprised at how much his rejection bothered her. She'd worked as a reporter at home in New York for several years and having a potential subject of an article resent her questions wasn't that unusual.

So why did Eli's coolness bother her so much?

She had no answers. Frustrated, she rolled onto her side and closed her eyes, determined to not think about him anymore.

But when she finally fell asleep, she dreamed of a tall, black-haired man with green eyes.

* * *

Eli woke to the sound of knuckles rapping on the hall door of the Lodge office, accompanied by Cade's voice.

"Hey, Eli. You in there?"

"Yeah, come on in." He sat up as Cade entered. "Is the party over?" He scrubbed his hands over his face, trying to wake.

"Everyone's gone, except for Zach, Mariah, Cynthia and me," Cade confirmed. "It's nearly midnight. Come join us in the kitchen."

"Sure." Eli stood, hearing bones crack as he stretched, yawning. Fully awake, he followed Cade down the hall and into the kitchen.

The big room was brightly lit, stainless-steel appliances and the polished floor's black-and-white tiles gleaming. The quick efficiency he'd noticed in the chef and her helpers earlier was obvious in the kitchen's appearance. Gone was the earlier clutter of platters, stemware and food—now everything was spotlessly clean, the counters neat and tidy.

Mariah and Cynthia perched on the tall stools at the island counter, their gowns bright splashes of crimson and blue in the black-and-white kitchen. Both women were barefoot; their stiletto-heeled sandals lay tumbled on the floor beneath their seats.

"Hey, Eli. Want dessert?" Zach lifted the tray he carried in one hand. It was loaded with miniature iced cakes.

Cynthia swiveled on her seat. "We were all so busy circulating that we barely touched the buffet, so we're making up for it now."

"Sounds good. Count me in." He took a seat across

the island counter from Cade as his brother settled onto the empty stool next to Mariah. "How was the party?" he asked.

"The media people were impressed, so I'm counting it a success," Zach said, his eyes glinting with satisfaction.

"Everyone I talked with said they loved the way you restored the Lodge," Mariah commented. "In fact, an older couple from California told me it looked exactly as they remembered it."

"That must have been Nico Tomaselli and his wife," Zach told her. "He's a movie producer who was a friend of Mom and Dad's and stayed at the Lodge in the old days."

"So many people asked about reservation information that I lost track of how many cards I gave out," Cynthia said with a laugh. "I think we're a hit."

"I'll drink to that." Mariah lifted her glass.

"You're toasting our success with milk?" Zach asked her in disbelief.

"I had enough champagne earlier," she told him with a twinkle.

"Which was really good, by the way," Cade told Cynthia. "I think you should keep that supplier."

"I'll make a note," she told him as she slipped down from her stool and walked to the fridge. "He has great imported ale, too."

"Now, that's what I'm talkin' about," Zach told her. "Champagne and wine are okay but real men drink beer, right, Cade?"

Eli sat quietly, a half smile on his face as he listened to his brothers tease the two women. He hadn't wanted to return to Montana but he couldn't deny he'd missed the good-natured harassment that always happened when his brothers got together.

"What are you drinking, Eli?" Cade asked.

"I'll have a beer."

Cade snagged another bottle out of the fridge and returned to the counter, sliding the bottle across the tiled top to Eli. "Here you go. Did you eat earlier?"

Eli nodded as he twisted off the bottle cap. "The chef grilled a steak and added a baked potato and salad. Great food."

"That's Jane," Cynthia said with pride. "She's a fabulous cook."

"Damned straight." Cade looked at Mariah. "Between Jane and Mariah's boss at the café, who makes the best desserts in three counties, Indian Springs is turning into gourmet land."

Zach laughed, Mariah and Cynthia joining him.

"Gourmet land?" Eli said with a bemused grin. "Did I make a wrong turn somewhere? This is the Triple C, right?"

"Yeah, it's the Triple C, but a lot of things have changed since we were all here last," Zach said.

Smiles disappeared and faces grew solemn. The kitchen suddenly seemed full of the ghosts of memories, not all of which were good, or happy.

"I suppose now's as good a time as any to talk about Dad's will, Eli," Cade said. "You'll need to see Ned Anderson, the estate attorney, tomorrow to get the official version, but basically, Dad left the Triple C to all of us, share and share alike. But he left specific parts of it to each of us that are ours alone. As Zach told you when you called from Spain, he left you Mom's studio and the contents."

"I'm still having trouble believing it," Eli told him. "It would be easier to accept that the world had just shifted on its axis and was spinning upside down." He shook his head, frowning first at Cade, then Zach, looking for explanations. "He blamed us for Mom's death. And he hated my artwork. When I was ten, he threatened to lock me in the cabin's cellar if he caught me drawing. Why would he give me her studio?"

"I know it doesn't sound logical." Cade's deep voice held a wealth of understanding. "Zach and I had the same reaction when we found out about Dad's will." He nodded at Zach. "He left the Lodge to Zach and the cattle to me. Brodie gets the horses."

Eli's gaze sharpened. "What horses?"

"We're not sure, but we think the Kigers might still be up on Tunk Mountain," Zach answered. "We haven't ridden out there to check yet."

"And we won't until Brodie comes home," Cade said. "I figure he should decide when and how he wants to deal with what Dad left him."

"From the brief info you gave me on the phone, it doesn't sound likely Brodie will be able to check whether the Kigers are in the far pasture," Eli said. "Even four-wheel drive can't make it through that rough country, at least not all the way to Tunk Mountain, and Brodie might not be able to sit a horse."

Cade shook his head, worry creasing lines beside his mouth. "Hard to say whether he will or not. The doctors say he won't, but Brodie says he will."

"Then he will," Eli said with easy conviction. "You know Brodie. He's never let anyone tell him what he can or can't do."

"I sure as hell hope you're right," Zach said with feeling.

"So am I." Eli couldn't conceive of a world in which his brother wasn't sitting a horse, chasing cattle or riding rodeo. It was impossible to comprehend. "I guess we'll know when he gets here. Which is…when?" He looked at each of the four in turn and registered the worried glances they exchanged. "Don't tell me he isn't coming home."

"We're not sure," Cade said with a sigh. "Zach and I went to see him in the convalescent center in California. Brodie agreed to come home only after Zach promised to find a way to break the will if Brodie didn't want to stay on the Triple C after he'd checked in with us."

"Not that I can actually do that," Zach put in, thrusting his hands through his hair to rake the heavy black strands away from his face. "The will is airtight. None of us can sell the land without all four agreeing."

"Even if one of us wanted to sell," Eli mused aloud. "Or even if one of us had enough money to buy out one of the others."

"Hell," Cade said with disgust. "If any one of us had enough money to buy out the others, we could use it to pay off the inheritance taxes."

"How much are they?" Eli asked.

"A little over two million dollars," Zach said succinctly.

"Holy…" Eli whistled, long and low, an audible expression of shock.

"So…I'm guessing by your reaction that you don't have that much sitting in your bank account," Cade said dryly.

"I wish." Eli shook his head. "My savings took a hit

when I spent a year interning with Lucan, but even before that, I couldn't have swung two mil. How are we going to come up with that much money?"

"We're hoping each of us will find a way to maximize what Dad left us and raise part of the money. Cade sold cattle and earned enough to meet the first payment. I'm projecting income off the Lodge over the next six months will bring in enough to make the second payment," Zach told him. "If you can find a way to generate income from whatever you find when you open Mom's studio, then we're three-quarters of the way to resolving the tax situation. And if Brodie comes home..."

"Wait." Eli held up his hand. "Haven't you and Cade already been in Mom's studio?"

"No," Cade said, his deep voice quiet. "The studio is yours, just like the Lodge is Zach's. I thought it only fair that you be the first to go in."

"And I agree," Zach said, his voice just as quietly convinced.

Eli lifted the bottle to his lips and drank, giving himself time to wash away the emotion that blocked his throat. "I didn't realize you literally meant you were leaving first contact to each of us." He wasn't sure he wanted to be the first person entering the studio where his mother had been working moments before she died. Nonetheless, he thought grimly, he'd do what needed to be done. "I'll do that tomorrow after I've seen the attorney. I'm assuming it's still locked. Do one of you have the keys?"

Cade nodded. "I picked them up from the attorney right after I talked to you. They're up at the house."

Eli looked over the faces of the four seated at the counter. "Is that where we're all staying? At the house?"

"I'm officially using my old room," Zach told him with a grin. "But I spend a lot of time at Cynthia's place in town."

Eli glanced at the pretty blonde, surprised when color bloomed in her cheeks. She met his gaze without flinching, however, and he guessed she didn't care that he knew she and Zach were semi-living together, even though she blushed at Zach's statement.

"And I'm down at the cabin with Mariah," Cade put in. "We're all in and out of the house on most days, though, since I'm still using Dad's office to run the Triple C, Zach's using his old room on occasion, and Mariah's been doing the housework."

Eli nodded. "Sounds good. You two want to open the studio with me?"

"Yeah," Zach responded, his expression somber. "I'm there."

Cade nodded when Eli looked at him, his eyes equally grave.

"Good." His brief acceptance closed the subject. "On another subject, I met a woman at the party tonight. She told me she's writing a book about Mom."

"Geez," Zach groaned.

"Was her name Amanda Blake?" Mariah asked.

"Yes." Eli raised an eyebrow. "Do you know her?"

"She's been in the café where I work and I've waited on her. She seems nice enough."

"No matter how nice she seems," Cade growled, "I don't want her poking around in our lives."

"Me, either." Zach's voice was clipped. "She drove out here and talked to us. As soon as we heard what she wanted, we told her we didn't have any comment. After she left, I looked her up online. Her credentials checked out—she's a reporter and editor for an art magazine in New York City. I read a couple of her articles online and the woman can write, but that doesn't change a thing. I don't want her writing a book about life on the Triple C."

Zach didn't add that he didn't want a writer telling the world about Joseph Coulter's alcoholism and the hell that life became on the ranch after their mother died. Eli agreed. He and his brothers had walked away from the chaos their father had created. None of them wanted their personal pain documented and exposed in a book for outsiders to read.

"I thought her name was familiar," Eli said, his memory jogged by Zach's comments. "She contacted my agent last year about an interview but I was in Spain and told him to put her off. She apparently has solid credentials and, given her background, knows where to look for all the details about Mom's art career. I seem to remember she has a sister who married the owner of a major gallery in New York, so she's got connections. My agent gave me that bit of information when he was trying to talk me into doing a phone interview with her. Regardless of her background, it's nobody's business but ours what happened after Mom died," Eli agreed grimly. "I don't want anyone nosing around, stirring up trouble." No matter how much he'd been drawn to her, he added silently. Circumstances meant Amanda Blake was off-limits.

"Your mother's art has skyrocketed in popularity over the last ten years or so," Cynthia put in. "It's not surprising there's interest in her life story. I'm wondering if there may be a way to use Ms. Blake to control what the public learns about your lives after your mother died."

"Are you saying you think we should cooperate with Amanda Blake?" Zach asked, a frown creasing his brow.

"I'm only suggesting you might want to consider telling her just enough to deflect her curiosity and keep her from digging more deeply into your family history." Cynthia laid her hand on Zach's arm.

Eli mentally shook his head as Zach seemed to calm under Cynthia's touch. The subtle influence the pretty blonde had on his brother was flat-out amazing, especially given Zach's fiercely independent nature.

"Maybe we should think about whether we could find a middle ground," he commented aloud. "If she's going to be asking questions in Indian Springs, then finding a way to distract her with some information— not all the truth, but enough to satisfy her—might not be a bad idea."

"Maybe," Cade responded, clearly not convinced. "I'll have to think about it."

"Good enough," Eli said.

Beside Zach, Cynthia yawned. "Sorry," she apologized. "We've been up since dawn, making sure all the details for the Lodge opening were taken care of, and I think the lack of sleep just caught up with me."

Eli glanced at his watch, mentally calculating how long it had been since he'd slept in a real bed. *Too long,* he thought. "I've been catnapping in airports and on planes for a few days myself. I think I'll head up to the house." He popped the miniature piece of chocolate cake into his mouth, pushed back the stool and stood.

"What time do you want to meet me with the keys at Mom's studio, Cade?"

"Why don't you give me a call on my cell when you get back from talking with Anderson?"

"Sounds good." Eli looked at Zach. "Does that work for you?"

"Sure. I'll be here at the Lodge. Cade can call me after he talks to you."

"Great." He looked at Cynthia and Mariah. "Nice to meet you, ladies. I'm guessing I'll probably see you tomorrow."

"There's a very good chance," Mariah told him.

"Come have lunch, or dinner, here at the Lodge," Cynthia said. "Jane keeps an open kitchen for the family."

"Sounds great. Good night, all." Eli glanced back to raise a hand in response to the chorus of good-nights and was struck by the picture of the two couples. There was a sense of rightness about his brothers, seated next to the women they'd chosen. His brothers loomed, dark-haired and broad-shouldered, next to their future brides with their blond hair and smaller female bodies. He'd never thought any of his brothers would marry, let alone look so perfectly content paired with a woman. But there was no mistaking the way the couples seemed to fit.

He was happy for his brothers but he knew he'd never join them. The concept of caring so much for a woman that he'd never want to leave her, would commit to spending the rest of his life with her, was as alien as the probability that invaders from outer space might land a UFO in the ranch pasture. And about as likely to happen, he thought. Just thinking about the remote possibility that he'd ever need a woman that badly made him want to run for the nearest exit.

Shaking his head in amazement, he walked down the hallway, crossed the dimly lit lobby and left the Lodge.

Lanterns were spaced down the length of the porch and their muted light spilled down the walkway to the parking area. Once Eli stepped into his truck and drove away from the Lodge, however, he was instantly surrounded by dark night. The truck's headlamps cut a swath of light across the gravel road ahead of him, illuminating the grassy shoulder on either side. But beyond the pickup's beams, only moon- and starlight eased the darkness. The cluster of ranch buildings loomed ahead, bulky black shapes relieved only by the single porch lights above the doors of the bunkhouse and ranch house.

Eli swung the pickup in a wide arc and parked in front of the house. Switching off the engine and grabbing his bag from the passenger seat, he stepped out of the truck.

The solid thunk of the pickup door closing was loud in the still, quiet night. Eli paused, turning in a half circle to sweep the skyline, taking in the bulk of black buttes rising against the starlit backdrop. A quarter moon gave scant light, but it was enough to sketch the ranch and its surroundings in black shadow and silver highlights.

Home. The word came unbidden, settling into his consciousness and deep into his bones, calming a restlessness he hadn't known lived within him.

He'd traveled a lot of miles since he'd left the Triple C, Eli thought. But in none of the places he'd landed had he ever felt this deep connection. It was as if a fraying line between his heart and the land was suddenly solid again, pulling taut and strong, anchoring him to this place.

He stood silent for a long moment, breathing in the scents of sage and fresh air, before he shook himself and stirred to walk to the house.

"Too damn tired," he muttered as he crossed the porch and pushed the unlocked door inward. "I'm imagining things."

He flipped the light switch to the right of the door and lamps came on in the living room.

The room was quiet, homey with the soft glow of lamplight over the deep-cushioned leather sofa and chairs, the polished wooden floors and the fireplace with its heavy oak mantel.

The last time he'd seen the room had been the morning he'd driven away from the Triple C. Joseph Coulter had stood in the center, fury on his face, and told his four sons that if they left, they couldn't come back until they knew he was dead.

Eli couldn't help but wonder if his father had known he was predicting their future.

And he couldn't help but wonder what the hell had made the old man leave everything he owned to the sons he'd spent years hating.

It was a question with no answer.

Eli hit the switch, shrouding the big room in darkness once again, and climbed the stairs, memory making him sure-footed as he moved down the upstairs hallway to a room near the end.

When he flicked on the light here, he felt as if he'd stepped back in time. Nothing about his old room had changed. A poster of Van Gogh's *Starry Night* was tacked on the wall above the desk. Next to it was a poster from the Daniels County Fair, listing Brodie as a rodeo competitor.

He dropped his bag on the heavy nineteenth-century oak chair next to the bed. Unbuttoning his shirt, he shrugged out of it, hung it over the back of the chair and sat on the edge of the bed to pull off his boots and socks. Standing once again, he unsnapped his jeans and shoved them down his legs and off before laying them over the chair seat.

The scent of clean sheets and fabric softener reached him as he pulled back the sheets. He suspected either Mariah or Cynthia had put fresh sheets on his bed and he made a mental note to thank them tomorrow. Then he snapped off the light, slid between the sheets and closed his eyes.

The Technicolor image of thick-lashed hazel eyes, dark hair and smooth skin instantly flooded him. He wondered hazily if Amanda Blake's soft eyes and lush mouth were going to haunt him from now on, but then sleep caught him, pulling him down into soft, welcome blackness.

Chapter Three

Despite the weariness that had sucked him into sleep the night before, Eli woke just after eight o'clock the following morning. He'd forgotten to close the blinds and he squinted against the bright sunlight that poured through the windows before tossing the bedcovers back and rising.

He showered and shaved, then headed downstairs to make coffee in the quiet kitchen. The refrigerator yielded a plastic container of fried chicken and he ate three pieces while standing at the sink, staring out the window. From his vantage point, he could see the back-yard, with the tall old maple tree in the far corner, the fence that marked the house area's boundaries, and the pasture that stretched toward the buttes rising not far away.

Once again, he felt the tug of familiarity and a sense of homecoming.

Maybe what he'd felt last night hadn't been only the result of a lack of sleep and the late hour, he thought.

The coffeemaker beeped, and he washed his hands, returned the chicken container to the fridge, then opened the cabinet over the coffeemaker. As he'd hoped, the cupboard held a variety of cups and mugs. He filled a thermal mug with strong black coffee and left the house.

It was just after 9:30 a.m. when he reached Indian Springs, and his meeting with the attorney lasted less than an hour. He left Ned Anderson's office with an envelope filled with copies of legal documents and paused on the sidewalk outside.

He glanced at his watch and realized that it was too early for lunch, but despite the chicken he'd eaten earlier, his stomach felt empty. He was considering crossing the street to the Indian Springs Café when a small car pulled into an empty parking slot just in front of the eatery. Amanda Blake stepped out, a file tucked under her arm and a purse slung over her shoulder. She disappeared inside the café.

I wonder where she's been and who she interrogated this morning.

With sudden decisiveness, he crossed the street and pulled open the door to the café.

The bells hanging on the inside of the glass panel chimed as the door swung closed behind him. He paused, scanning the room with its center tables ringed by booths lining the outer walls. Amanda was seated in a booth toward the back, her head bent as she studied the menu.

He wound his way around the tables and slid onto the seat opposite her.

Amanda looked up from the menu when someone sat down across from her, the list of pies immediately forgotten as she realized the man was Eli Coulter. "Good morning, Eli." She hesitated only a second before continuing. "I'm surprised to see you here."

His eyes crinkled at the corners as he smiled, clearly amused. "Here in Indian Springs—or here in your booth?"

"Both, actually." Her fingers curled tighter on the edges of the vinyl-covered menu, reacting to his charm.

"I had to check in with the estate attorney this morning. His office is just across the street and when I left there, I saw you park and come in here." He glanced around the half-full café, then back at her. "Since I was hungry, I thought I'd come over and join you."

"You did?" Her voice rose in disbelief. She stared at him but his expression was innocently friendly. "Why would you..." She paused as the waitress arrived. Amanda placed her order for rhubarb-strawberry pie and coffee, waiting impatiently while Eli did the same and the woman left before she continued. "I had the distinct impression last night that you didn't want to talk to me again. In fact, I assumed after our conversation that you'd be avoiding me like the plague. So why are you sitting at my booth?"

"Maybe I realized this morning that I might have been a little cranky last night and might need to apologize for being rude."

An apology was the last thing she'd expected. She studied his face before slowly shaking her head. "While it's nice to hear, I don't believe for a minute that you didn't mean what you said. Because your brothers clearly don't want me writing about your mother either. Only they were a little more polite when they refused to help me," she added. "So tell me the real reason you're here."

Amanda thought she saw surprise and brief admiration flash across his features before he answered.

"It's not my practice to be rude to guests in my family's company, and the apology for that is sincere. But that's not what brought me in here. I saw you across the street and wondered who you'd been interrogating this morning." He shrugged. "Chalk it up to curiosity."

She rolled her eyes, annoyed with his reasons but pleased he'd been honest.

"I wasn't interviewing anyone—I was at the library reading newspaper archives. Why do you and your brothers dislike reporters so much?" she asked bluntly.

"Because our experience with them hasn't been good," he told her.

She tilted her head, clearly puzzled, but didn't demand he elaborate. Because she didn't push, he decided to tell her.

"We were kids when Mom died, but for several weeks, reporters swarmed us every time we went into town. Dad made a rule that we had to stay together but it was hard to do. Eventually, each of us was confronted—none of us were safe. Three reporters for a celebrity gossip magazine caught me alone outside the drugstore and grilled me about the details of Mom's death. By the time they were done, I was so confused that I had no idea what I'd told them." Eli heard Amanda's gasp of outrage but continued. "I was nine years old. What did I know about fielding reporters' questions?" He shrugged. "They concocted a bunch of lies, wrote the story as if it were truth, and gossip columns in the arts sections of city newspapers picked up the story and spread it everywhere. Dad grounded me for the entire summer."

"But that wasn't fair," Amanda exclaimed. "You were just a child."

"He'd told us never to get separated when we were in town. I broke a rule."

She frowned at him and opened her mouth to speak but he continued before she could argue further.

"The fallout from that story never really went away. When I followed my mother into the same field, her art and life inevitably came up. And just as inevitably, I kept being asked questions about that same damned story." His smile was cynical. "Reporters' articles never go away. They live forever on the internet. And that," he told her with conviction, "is why I don't trust reporters." *Or just about anyone else who seems interested in Mom's life,* he thought grimly.

Amanda was appalled. She could only imagine how being hounded while grieving his mother's death had scarred the little boy Eli had been.

"No wonder you have a negative view of reporters," she said. "I doubt it will change your mind but for the record, I've never pursued children to get a story. Nor would I," she added firmly. "It's unethical—not to mention immoral."

A faint smile lit his eyes. "I'm glad to hear you say that. It's good to know someone in the press has ethics."

"I looked you up on the internet last night," she told him. "I found a brief bio on your agent's website, but beyond that, there wasn't a lot of information."

He nodded just as their waitress returned with their drinks and pie. He waited until she'd left before continuing. "I'm happy to let my agent field any requests for publicity. I gave a few interviews in the beginning but after being misquoted more than once, I avoid talking to the press." He picked up his fork, pointing it at her. "For the record, this is *not* going to show up in your book, right?"

Amanda laughed. "You look so ferocious, threatening me with your fork."

He glanced at the fork, then back at her, and shrugged. His green eyes lit with warmth and self-deprecation. "Not a very effective weapon, is it?"

"No, I'm afraid not."

And with that, the last of the wary animosity between them seemed to evaporate. In tacit acceptance of the truce between them, they chatted for the next hour over coffee, although each carefully kept their comments general.

Nonetheless, when they left the restaurant, Amanda found herself wishing he was an ordinary guy and not part of her research. She liked him, she thought as she slid into her car and watched him jog across the street to climb into a pickup truck. She had no illusions that their sharing a booth and chatting had permanently changed his view of her. It felt more as if he'd called a temporary truce, and she suspected that the next time they met, he would likely still be suspicious of her motives.

She'd never expected to meet someone like him on this trip and her attraction to him complicated matters. With a sigh, she started her car and backed out of the parking space.

Regardless of how much she was drawn to Eli Coulter, she still had work to do, she told herself firmly.

Despite her best efforts to concentrate solely on

her research, however, thoughts of Eli smiling as he sprawled opposite her in the café booth kept intruding.

Eli spent the half-hour drive back to the ranch trying to figure out what it was about Amanda that made him tell her things he usually kept to himself.

Was it the warm interest in her hazel eyes that lured him into opening up and confiding in her?

He reached the ranch house, no closer to understanding the effect she had on him. He went inside and when he found the house empty, tossed the packet of legal documents on the table and left again to search for his brothers.

Just as he stepped off the porch, Cade rounded the corner of the barn and walked toward him.

"Hey," Eli called as his brother neared. "Did you bring the keys?"

"Yeah." Cade lifted his hand, a set of metal keys on a round metal ring dangling from his fingers. "Are you ready to do this?"

"As ready as I'll ever be," Eli told him, accepting the key ring and shoving it in his jeans pocket. "Where's Zach?"

"He's meeting us at the studio."

The two men climbed into Eli's truck and left the ranch yard, following the gravel road for a quarter mile before turning into a dirt drive that led off the road and beneath the thick green leaves of towering maple trees. Zach was already there, leaning against the front bumper of his pickup, arms crossed. He straightened as Eli parked next to him, joining Cade to follow Eli up the short walk to the single-story studio's front door.

"I pulled the plywood off the doors and windows."

Zach pointed to a stack of wood on one side of the walk. "The Lodge had all the windows covered when we went in and we couldn't see a damned thing. I figured ripping the wood off would save some time."

"Thanks." Eli fitted one of the keys into the lock. Stiff from years of being unused, metal grated against metal before the lock mechanism turned and slid free. Eli pocketed the keys and opened the door, shoving it inward and stepping over the threshold.

He brushed his hand over the light switch beside the door frame but got no response.

"Electricity isn't working," he commented as he halted just inside, his gaze sweeping slowly over the interior.

Cade and Zach joined him, as silent as he as they studied the big room.

Despite being closed and shuttered for more than two decades, the area was surprisingly undamaged. Tools hung neatly on the wall above the long workbench, where welding equipment sat next to a vise that held a curved piece of blackened metal. The white-painted walls were hung with sculptures in various stages of completion, the silver and copper metal black with tarnish and draped with ghostly swathes of cobwebs. A thick layer of dust coated every surface in the long room and the silence was eerie.

"Looks better than the Lodge did when we opened it," Zach commented.

"I don't see water damage, so with any luck, the roof's still sound," Cade agreed. "And there's no sign of the mice and raccoon problems we found at the Lodge."

Eli pointed at the floor, where mice droppings were scattered in the dust. "Mice have been in here. Most everything in the building is wood or metal, though, so there's probably not much they could destroy."

The three walked farther into the room. The bungalow space was divided into a small bathroom and storage room to the left of the entry, while the remainder was one long, open room. At the far end, most of the wall was taken up by a stone fireplace, built of smooth river rocks. A small corner kitchenette held an apartment-size range, refrigerator and cupboards. The side of the building facing the lawn that sloped down to the creek had French doors.

Eli steeled himself to look at the glass-paned doors, which opened out onto a wide deck with shallow steps that led down to the lawn and the creek beyond. It was there his mother had leaned, laughing at him and his brothers as they played in the water on that fateful day. They'd teased her into joining them and she'd impulsively grabbed the rope tied to a limb on the old tree, swinging out over the water to join them. She'd hit her head on a half-submerged rock and died from the injury within days.

He yanked his thoughts away from his mother's death and stepped farther into the room, moving to the long worktable.

Behind him, Cade and Zach walked forward as well.

"I've wondered if Mom left any finished pieces in here," Zach commented. "But it doesn't look like it."

Eli looked over his shoulder, turning in a slow half circle to scan the room. "Lots of unfinished sculptures hanging on the walls," he said. "But she always stored the final pieces in the vault when she was done working on them."

"The vault?" Zach's eyebrows rose, his eyes questioning. "She had a vault?"

"Sure. Don't you remember?" Cade joined Eli and paused, hands on hips as he looked around the room, a faint frown on his face. "She and Dad argued about the cost but Dad finally gave in. What I don't remember, though, is where it's located."

"It's behind the fireplace." Eli strode the length of the room, dust puffing upward from beneath his boots.

"Why don't I know this?" Zach asked, following him.

"Mom had it put in the summer you two went with Dad to visit the McClouds in Wolf Creek. You were gone a week, and when you came back, it was already installed."

Eli reached the fireplace, counted rocks to the left of the mantel edge, three over and four down, and pressed the heel of his hand against a smooth white stone. The stone moved inward with a groan, a grating noise loud in the room as a panel swung outward.

"Well, I'll be damned." Cade stared at the inky opening. "How far in does it go?"

"The anteroom is small, maybe enough space for four or five people. Plenty of room to stand while you dial in the combination for the lock."

"Dial in the combination?" Zach peered into the darkness. "How old is this vault? Nobody uses dial locks anymore."

"Mom wanted an old-fashioned vault with tumblers. I'm sure she had a reason but I can't remember what it was," Eli replied.

"She probably just wanted an old-fashioned safe,"

Cade commented. "She always chose antiques, if she could get them."

"Makes sense," Zach agreed. "God knows, she collected a ton of other antiques." He moved toward the door. "I'll get the flashlight from my truck so we can go inside."

He was back short moments later. Eli took the flashlight and switched it on, stepping through the opening. His brothers followed.

The room was bigger than Eli had remembered, with enough space for perhaps a half dozen people to stand. He swept the flashlight's beam over the wall opposite the entry and found his memory about the vault was correct. The entire wall was a heavy black metal door with a large combination lock and solid handle just left of center. Gold paint scrolled around the edges of the huge door.

"Somebody must have salvaged this out of an old bank," he commented, stepping closer to run his fingertips over the round combination lock that was as big as his palm.

"That would be my guess," Cade agreed.

"The question is, how the hell do we get it open?" Zach asked. "If we can't find the combination, we'll have to hire a locksmith to drill out the lock."

"Mom had a thing about letters and numbers," Eli said slowly. "Remember the games she used to play with us?"

"She used the first letters of our names and their number in the alphabet," Cade said, recognition dawning. "She loved those games."

"Yeah, and if I remember right…" Eli walked out of the small hidden room and crossed to the worktable.

"She hid the combination in plain sight." He brushed off a 1920s mechanic's vise clamped to the edge of the table, then used his thumb to rub away the dust filling the grooves of a set of numbers etched into the side. To the casual observer, the numbers looked like an identification for the vise. But they meant something else to Eli. "And here it is." He memorized the short set of numbers and returned to the hidden room to spin the dial. The tumblers clicked audibly into place, and he lowered the handle, pulling the door open. The big door moved ponderously, the hinges protesting with squeals and creaks.

Cade handed the flashlight to Eli and gestured him forward. Eli stepped into the vault, his brothers close behind.

He whistled, a long, low exclamation of surprise.

The vault door concealed a room at least ten feet square, with concrete walls and floor. Heavy metal shelves were bolted to one wall and held a collection of silver and copper sculptures. Opposite the shelves, two strongboxes sat on the floor. Hung on the wall above them were a dozen or more medium to large sculptures of mustangs, antelope, deer, eagles and hawks.

Eli moved slowly along the wall, brushing his fingertips over the tarnished silver and copper of manes and tails until he reached the strongboxes. Bending, he slipped the latch on the first one and lifted the lid.

Stunned, he went down on his heels and stared at the interior of the box. Stacked neatly inside were wrapped bars of silver. He leaned over and slipped the latch of the second strongbox, lifting the lid to reveal the gleam of copper.

"Damn." Cade's stunned voice sounded behind him. "Is that what I think it is?"

"Yeah," Eli confirmed. "Silver and copper. Probably worth a fortune in today's market."

"Two million?" Zach asked hopefully.

Eli shook his head. "Unfortunately, no."

He rose and crossed to the shelving, glutting his senses on the graceful curves and angles of his mother's work. "She was amazing," he muttered, once again trailing a finger over the curvature of a mustang's copper back. "Absolutely amazing."

"Dad couldn't have known what was in this vault," Cade said. "Mariah said he barely made a living those last few years."

"Doesn't make sense that he wouldn't have sold some of this to keep the Triple C in better shape," Zach put in.

Eli agreed. "Only a few of these pieces are finished, but a Melanie Coulter sculpture in today's marketplace, even unfinished, would have given him added income over the years—probably enough to live comfortably. So why didn't he do it?" he mused as he slowly assessed the contents of the vault.

"He didn't sell anything," Cade said. "It's as if the ranch and everything on it were frozen in time when Mom died."

"Certainly after we left," Eli agreed. "My room even has the same posters on the wall and my old boots on the floor in the closet." He shrugged, trying to shake off the sadness and confusion that hung like a shadow in the room. "I doubt we'll ever know all the reasons he did what he did. All we can do is try and sort out what's left." He waved a hand, indicating the shelves, walls and the two strongboxes. "I need to take a thorough inventory, but off the top of my head, I'm guessing there's a way to maximize the value of what we've found here."

"Do you think selling everything will pay off the taxes?" Zach asked.

"Probably not." Eli shook his head. "Especially not if we call a dealer and tell him we're dropping all this on the market at once. Mom's sculptures are valuable, but that's partly because so few of them ever come up for sale. If we flood the market with what's in this vault, we stand a good chance of making the value drop like a rock."

"So we've got a lot of value here but we can't sell it? What's the answer?" Cade frowned, his gaze locked on Eli.

"I don't know yet. Let me think about it." Eli took a wooden box from a shelf and lifted the lid. "Look at these," he said, his voice reverent as he stared at six intricately worked platinum rings, each set with a different gem.

"I didn't know Mom made jewelry," Zach said.

"She didn't make a lot. She preferred working with bigger designs, bigger pieces, but there are a few necklaces, bracelets and rings owned by collectors." Eli frowned, trying to remember what he'd learned about his mother's work. He'd been too young when she died to fully understand her body of work, but as an adult, he'd made a point of studying her collections. "Any jewelry by her is so rare that I think they must have been custom pieces, made for special clients. I didn't know there were any here, uncirculated. The rings are all versions of the same design, almost as if she was practicing, see?" He held up one of the rings between forefinger and thumb.

Zach bent closer, nodding as he studied the delicate, graceful circle with its golden brown stone.

"She was an amazing artist," Cade commented. "That's beautiful. The color of the stone reminds me of Mariah's eyes in the sunlight."

Eli looked up. "It's a brown topaz." He scanned the remaining five rings tucked into the black velvet lining of the small box. "And this one is almost the same color as Cynthia's eyes, isn't it, Zach?" With sudden decision, he handed the first ring to Cade and lifted the second one from its velvet nest. "I didn't notice engagement rings on Cynthia's and Mariah's fingers last night, so I'm guessing you two haven't got around to giving them one yet. I want you to take these."

"Are you serious?" Zach took the ring from Eli and stared at the curved platinum circle with its large blue topaz stone.

"Yeah. Mom would do the same, if she were here." Eli was convinced he'd done the right thing when Cade and Zach exchanged a glance, both men clearing their throats.

"Thanks, Eli. If you're sure you want us to have them, I'd be proud to have Mariah wear a ring made by Mom." Cade's deep voice rasped with emotion.

"Same for me and Cynthia, Eli." Zach's voice held the same throb of emotion.

"Good." Eli closed the small wooden box lid with an audible snap.

"That leaves four more for you and Brodie to choose from when you get engaged," Zach told him, only half teasing.

"Yeah, right," Eli said dryly. "I'll save mine to give to your daughters on their sixteenth birthday."

"I'm only having sons," Cade answered promptly. "Little girls terrify me. They wear pink ribbons, and when they're teenagers, boys hang around."

"I'm with Cade," Zach said with feeling. "The possibility scares the hell out of me."

Eli clapped his hand on Zach's shoulder. "Now you know how the fathers of all those girls you dated in high school felt."

Zach groaned and Eli chuckled when he felt him shudder.

They left the vault, locking it behind them and easing the concealing rock panel back into place.

"Amazing," Zach said, running a searching glance over the seamless fit of door and wall. "I know where the panel is but I can't see it."

The three left the studio, Eli stopping to lock the door before they walked to the trucks.

"Now what?" Zach asked.

Eli looked at Cade. His oldest brother stood easily, arms folded across his chest.

"I need some time to think." Eli's gaze left his brothers and found the tall rise of buttes on the horizon. "I'd like to spend a few nights out. Can I borrow Jiggs?"

"Sure." Cade nodded. "Camping gear is in the barn's tack room. If there aren't enough supplies at the house, Pete probably has all the food you'll need at the bunkhouse."

"Pete?" Eli asked.

"Pete Smith, one of the bachelor ranch hands," Zach told him. "The other is J. T. Butler."

"So who's working the ranch?" Eli looked from him

to Cade and back again. "Just you two and a couple of hired men?"

Cade grinned. "Just us two, plus a sixty-five-year-old, a high school kid and a married couple that came on board last month."

"You're kidding, right?"

"Nope." Zach laughed outright. "And that's exactly what I said when I first came home, practically word for word. We're managing, barely, with Pete, J.T. and John Arnold. The Turner boys are willing to help out when we need a bigger crew."

Arrested, Eli let himself be sidetracked at the mention of his old friends. "How are the Turners?"

"They're fine, and surprisingly enough, all of them are still living on their place," Cade told him.

"I'll have to look them up," Eli said. Years earlier the six Turner brothers had been orphaned when their parents' plane went down during a sudden storm. The oldest, Jed, had refused to let his brothers be separated, and though barely an adult himself, he'd managed to keep the ranch afloat and the brothers together. The six Turners and four Coulter brothers had been inseparable during school, growing up together, until Eli and his brothers left the Triple C when Eli was nineteen.

"They'll be glad to see you. Mason's been asking when you were expected," Zach told him. "You should give him a call."

"I'll do that," Eli said. "Right after I get back."

"When are you leaving?" Cade asked.

"As soon as I get a pack, a sleeping bag and some food."

"Come down to the Lodge and raid the kitchen if you need to," Zach told him, moving toward his truck.

"I'll do that. Thanks, Zach."

Zach raised a hand in farewell and opened the door to his pickup.

"While you're out, you can check the fence lines. I haven't had time to ride farther than the home pasture for the last few weeks. And you'd better take a couple of apples for Jiggs," Cade told Eli as they climbed into his pickup. "Mariah's spoiled him."

"Yeah?" Eli laughed. "Lucky horse."

They followed Zach out of the studio's driveway, Zach turning right toward the Lodge while Eli made a left to return to the ranch.

An hour later he rode away from the cluster of buildings. The black stallion carried a pack with camping gear tied behind the cantle. The saddle and bridle were Cade's, the 30-30 rifle shoved into the leather scabbard had hung in Joseph Coulter's office, and like his brothers, Eli wouldn't have ridden out without it. In an emergency, the rifle would mercifully end the suffering of an injured animal or signal for help if he himself had an accident. The enamel coffeepot and cups were from the bunkhouse and Eli remembered using them when he was a kid.

Just more of the many things that had stayed the same on the Triple C, he reflected as he leaned sideways in his saddle to open the gate blocking the lane into the pasture. He kneed Jiggs through the opening and closed the gate behind them before lifting the big horse into a ground-eating lope.

They climbed a rise and dropped down the other side, leaving the ranch buildings and any sign of humans behind as they moved deeper into the pasture, following a single cattle track that wound over the sage-dotted land ahead.

Once again, Eli felt the tug of the tie between him and the land he'd roamed as a child. The line held firm, strong and sure, settling him and easing the grief that had blindsided him as he'd stood in the studio among his mother's things.

Two days after seeing Eli at the cafe, Amanda woke early and left the hotel to go jogging. At barely 6:00 a.m., the sun was already gaining heat. The bright rays were warm on her arms and legs, bare below the midthigh hem of blue shorts and the straps of her white tank top. She'd pulled her long hair into a ponytail and tucked the ends through the back opening of a Yankees baseball cap, adding dark sunglasses to further protect her eyes. The business district surrounding the hotel on Main Street was quickly left behind for wide residential streets lined with tall old maple trees that stretched out their leafy green limbs to shade the sidewalks. The avenues were quiet and nearly empty, the driver of the occasional passing car waving and smiling. The first couple of times it happened, Amanda had been too startled to wave back, but after that, she responded in kind.

Just one of the perks of living in a small town, she thought, charmed by the friendly drivers.

Each morning since she'd arrived over a week ago, she'd jogged through the residential streets of the small town. Indian Springs was an interesting mix of turn-of-the-century Victorian homes that were beautifully preserved and stood proudly amid lush gardens edged by picket fences, and more contemporary ramblers with manicured lawns and flower beds. If there was a run-down section of Indian Springs, Amanda hadn't found it yet.

Forty-five minutes later she cut across the small, picturesque town park with its swing set, slide, sandbox and scattering of picnic tables near leafy maples and slowed to a walk. By the time she covered the remaining three blocks to reach the Indian Springs Café on Main Street, she was no longer breathing hard.

She pulled open the heavy plate-glass door and stepped inside. The café was crowded and noisy with the chatter and laughter of customers seated at tables and booths. Waitresses moved quickly, slipping easily around customers and chairs as they filled orders and topped off drinks.

"Good morning. Table or booth?"

Amanda recognized Mariah Jones from earlier visits to the café and returned her friendly smile. "Booth, please."

She followed the blonde waitress as she swiftly threaded her way around tables and customers to a booth near the back of the café.

"Here we go. Can I get you something to drink?"

"I'd love some coffee and a glass of ice water," Amanda told her, sliding into the booth and taking the vinyl-covered menu Mariah held out.

"I'll be right back."

Amanda was just closing the menu when Mariah returned with water and coffee.

"Ready to order?"

"Yes, thank you." Amanda watched Mariah whip a pad and pen out of the apron tied at her waist. "I'll have the house omelet with salsa and sourdough toast and..." Her voice stopped abruptly before she blurted out, "Oh. My. That's the most gorgeous ring I've ever seen."

Mariah flushed with pleasure, holding out her left hand to display a platinum ring set with a golden brown stone. "Thank you. Cade's mother designed it. Eli found several rings among her things and insisted Cade have it." She sighed, her expression dreamy. "I never imagined I'd have something so beautiful, and it's so absolutely perfect, almost as if she'd created it specifically for me."

"You're a lucky woman," Amanda told her with all sincerity. She knew from her research that Melanie Coulter had created very few pieces of jewelry. The few that existed were highly sought after by collectors.

"I know." Mariah smiled mistily. "Eli gave one to Zach for Cynthia, too. We have to do something special to thank him when he gets back."

"Back? Has he left the ranch?" Amanda was surprised at how disappointed she was that Eli was gone. Her research would likely be completed by the end of the week and she'd be leaving Indian Springs. She might not see him again.

"Just for a few days," Mariah told her. "And technically speaking, he hasn't left the Triple C. Cade says he's riding fence for a few days, but I suspect he just wanted to take Jiggs and go camping."

"Oh, I see." Amanda wasn't sure why she felt so relieved since it still wasn't likely she'd see Eli Coulter before she left town.

"Mariah, order up!" The cook's call carried over the noise in the room.

"Oops, gotta run. I'll be back with your omelet in a few minutes," Mariah said quickly, turning to hurry off.

Amanda nodded but Mariah was already gone.

The dreamy look on Mariah's face when she'd stared at her engagement ring was exactly like the expression Amanda's older sister, Lindsey, had worn when she displayed her engagement ring. Lindsey and Tom had been married for three years now and had a one-year-old daughter. Sometimes, Amanda mused, Lindsey had that same adoring look in her eyes when she looked at Tom or their daughter, Emma.

Amanda herself had never been engaged, but she recognized the connection between the promise of the ring and the love Lindsey felt for her small family. Clearly, Mariah felt the same about her fiancé.

Amanda was awed at the visual artistry of Melanie Coulter's work. The ring was one of a kind and stunningly beautiful.

And Mariah said Cynthia has one, too, Amanda thought with amazement.

She'd heard rumors that the Coulter brothers faced the possibility of losing the Triple C to inheritance taxes. Contrary to those rumors, if Melanie Coulter had left a collection of her art at the ranch, the brothers might be very rich men, indeed.

She'd give anything to see inside the studio on the ranch where Melanie had worked.

But that would never happen, she thought with a sigh. Eli had told her so, in no uncertain terms.

Much as she hated to abandon her plan, she clearly had to give up her hope that Melanie Coulter's sons would cooperate with her work on the biography of their mother. Instead, she'd have to be satisfied with interviewing the residents of Indian Springs.

She glanced at her watch. She had an appointment

with ninety-year-old Helen Cousins at 10:00 a.m. By the time she ate breakfast and returned to the hotel, showered and changed, then drove to the Cousins' ranch some ten miles from town, she calculated, it would be nearly ten.

A half hour later she left the café and walked briskly back to her hotel, determined to concentrate her energy and time on interviewing the local ranchers and townspeople who had known Melanie and Joseph Coulter personally.

She was just as determined to stop thinking about Eli Coulter. She was spending way too much time daydreaming about him.

But the memory of warm green eyes and an irresistible smile continued to pop into her mind at unexpected moments, surprising her and distracting her from whatever she was doing. Eli Coulter was never far from her thoughts.

Chapter Four

While Amanda was occupied with interviewing members of the Indian Springs ranching community over the next three days, Eli was riding the Triple C fence line and sleeping under the stars.

The long hours with only Jiggs for company gave him plenty of time to consider options for dealing with his mother's legacy.

That he had a legacy still seemed improbable. He couldn't understand why his father had given him Melanie's studio with its tools and what were surely her last, irreplaceable pieces of art. If the possibility had ever occurred to him, he would have bet Joseph would have burned the studio to the ground before he'd let Eli set foot in it.

What had happened to Joseph in the years after Eli and his brothers left the Triple C?

He could find no rational answers to the puzzle that

was his father, and at last, he pushed the questions aside to focus on how best to use his mother's last work to save the Triple C.

The solution came to him while he was repairing a line of barbed-wire fence, the sun beating down and sweat dampening the back of his T-shirt. He pondered the idea, considering it from all angles, thinking of all the negatives, while he worked on the fence. He thought about it some more, dissecting it piece by piece, considering the potential pitfalls, while he boiled coffee and heated rabbit stew over a campfire. And he lay awake long after dark, staring up at the glitter of stars hanging like jewels in the black night sky. Until at last, satisfied that it could work, he tipped his hat down over his face, pulled the sleeping bag up to his chin and went to sleep.

The next morning he broke camp before daybreak, saddled Jiggs and headed home. By 9:00 a.m. he'd turned Jiggs loose in the corral next to the barn and located Cade and Zach in the ranch house office.

"Hey, Eli," Cade greeted him when he stepped into the room. "When did you get back?"

"Just now." Eli hung his hat on the rack of deer antlers on the wall to the left of the door and took a seat, stretching his legs out and crossing his booted feet.

"You look like hell," Zach said with a grin. "Did you fix the fence above Ten Flats?"

"Thanks, and yeah, I fixed the fence."

"Good. That means I don't have to," Zach told him.

"Did you ride all the way in from Ten Flats this morning?" Cade asked.

Eli nodded. "I left before daybreak."

"I hope you gave Jiggs some oats when you got back," Cade said dryly. "That's a long ride."

"Not for Jiggs," Eli told him.

"He's tough," Cade agreed, a touch of pride and affection in his tone. "Did you have breakfast?"

"Just water and jerky. I wanted to get home."

"Did you?" Cade pushed a mug and the carafe of coffee across the desktop. He waited until Eli took his first sip. "You ready to tell us what's up?"

Eli took another drink of coffee. "I have a plan."

"Good. What is it?" Zach sat forward on the leather sofa.

"It involves using Amanda Blake."

"Oh, hell," Cade groaned.

"Hold on. Just hear me out." Eli swallowed another mouthful of coffee. "As I see it, this is the situation. To raise the maximum amount of money from the sculptures Mom left, I need to choose a limited number—let's say ten or twelve, or maybe as many as twenty—and find a gallery in New York that will agree to a showing followed by an auction. Collectors will be excited that a dozen or more previously unknown sculptures by Melanie Coulter are available. The fact that no one has seen them before will generate a lot of buzz."

"People will be interested in them even though some of them aren't finished?" Cade asked.

Eli nodded. "I think so. Quite a few pieces are complete and even those that are only partially finished are still unmistakably Mom's work."

"How will you find a gallery?" Zach asked. "Are you planning on using your agent and the place in San Francisco that sells your work?"

"I can certainly start with my agent and he may have some ideas, but I want the auction held at a gallery in

New York." Eli looked at his brothers. "Which brings us to the other half of my plan."

Cade's eyes narrowed. "Why is the alarm bell in my head ringing?"

"Probably because you aren't going to like what I'm about to suggest," Eli said with a wry grin. "But hear me out, okay?"

Cade and Zach both nodded.

"I think we can kill two birds with one stone. Because of her work at the magazine, Amanda Blake probably knows most of the movers and shakers in New York's art community. And like I told you earlier, her sister is married to the owner of the most prestigious gallery in the city. I suggest we make her an offer. She hooks us up with her brother-in-law and gets him to guarantee a showing within, say, two months. In return, we give her limited—*very* limited," he stressed, "access to some personal info about Mom. We can let Amanda read a few of her journals, look at some of the family photographs taken when we were kids, that kind of stuff. Nothing after Mom died. And she has to sign a binding contract that bans her from printing anything about any of us after the date of Mom's death."

"Would she do that?" Zach asked, dubious.

"She will if she wants access to Mom's things," Eli said grimly. "I'm guessing the chance to claim on the book jacket that we consented to give her access to personal, private family artifacts is worth a lot to her."

"I suppose it could work," Cade said slowly. "How long would she be around? And who's going to watch her?"

"I'll have to spend time in the studio, getting Mom's

work ready for the gallery. We can limit Amanda's access to the studio and only during the hours I'm there."

"She's going to know you're watching her," Zach said.

Eli shrugged. "I plan to tell her up front just what the deal is. I don't trust reporters and I've got no cause to think she's any different. But I'm not worried about letting her sit at a table in Mom's studio, looking at Mom's photos and reading a handful of daily journals, while I'm sitting a few feet away. What harm can she do?"

"If she's willing to sign a contract agreeing not to write about anything following the date of Mom's death, and you're willing to keep an eye on her, I guess the trade-off for her connections to get Mom's sculptures sold sounds good." Zach looked at Cade. "What do you think?"

"I'm not crazy about any plan that encourages a stranger to snoop into family business but given the situation…" Cade shrugged. "It's as good a plan as any. In fact, it's the only plan at the moment."

"I think it can work," Eli told them. "And if you two agree, I'll shower and head into town to talk to Amanda."

"I'm in," Zach said with decision.

"I wish we didn't have to do it, but…I'm in, too," Cade told him.

Eli nodded abruptly and rose to stride to the door. "I'll let you know what she says."

He left the office, the sound of his boots on the wooden floor echoing down the hall.

For a moment, Cade and Zach stared silently at the empty doorway.

"I hope to hell he knows what he's doing," Zach said softly.

"So do I." Cade's voice was grim.

Upstairs, Eli showered, shaved, pulled on clean jeans, boots and a white T-shirt, and then drove to Indian Springs. The town had two motels and a small hotel and he got lucky when he tried the hotel first.

The young woman behind the desk rang Amanda's room for him. He couldn't hear what Amanda said to the clerk, but the clerk advised him to wait.

It had probably only been a few minutes, but it seemed like an hour.

Just as he was about to give up, he heard footsteps behind him.

"Mr. Coulter." Amanda's voice was reserved; her expression wary.

She's probably wondering what the hell I'm doing here, he thought.

Eli flicked a quick glance over her. Her hair was pulled up in a ponytail and the ends looked damp. She was dressed in a narrow blue skirt and a white short-sleeved top, with dark blue earrings at her ears and blue-and-white bangles on her wrists. She looked cool and comfortable, right down to her bare feet, with toenails tipped in bright red polish visible in her sandals.

He realized he was staring and, given what she was wearing, he suspected she had been about to go out.

"Ms. Blake," he said, acknowledging her greeting. "Is this a bad time?"

Thick lashes lowered and lifted slowly as she blinked, clearly caught off guard by his question.

"That depends," she told him, hazel eyes apprehensive behind her narrow-framed glasses. "A bad time for what?"

"To have a talk." He gestured at her clothes. "If you're on your way somewhere, I can come back later."

She glanced down, smoothing her palm over the dark blue material at the curve of her hip. "I'm meeting the town librarian for lunch later. My treat, to say thank you for her help while I've been researching Indian Springs history. But that's not for another hour or two." She stepped back. "We can talk in my room."

Eli followed her upstairs and into her room. The bed was neatly made, a pair of dark blue heeled sandals sat on the carpet next to the nightstand. The air was fragrant with the floral scent of shampoo and soap. A small round table sat in front of the window, one of its two chairs pushed back and a laptop open atop the pale wood surface.

Behind him, Amanda closed the door before brushing past him to walk to the table. "We can sit here, if you'd like."

Eli followed her, holding her chair as she slipped into it before he settled into the other seat.

"Would you like some coffee?" she asked, lifting a white carafe and pouring.

"No, thanks." He took off his Stetson and set it on the tabletop.

"I hope you don't mind if I have some," she told him. "I haven't had my daily quota of caffeine yet this morning."

"Not at all." Now that he was here, Eli wasn't sure exactly how to start this conversation.

She eyed him over the rim of the cup as she sipped,

her gaze cautious but layered with curiosity. "So," she said. "What is it you wanted to talk about?"

Eli decided to be blunt.

"I have a proposal," he said without preliminaries. "One that would allow you to have access to some of my mom's personal information for your book."

Amanda's eyes widened and she lowered her cup to its saucer. "That would be wonderful," she said before her expression turned skeptical. "What do I have to do in return? Kill somebody?"

"No." A reluctant grin tugged at his lips. The New York girl was funny—and smart to be suspicious of his motives. "But you have to agree not to write anything about our family subsequent to Mom's death. And you have to get your brother-in-law to agree to an exhibit and auction of Melanie Coulter originals at his gallery."

Clearly surprised and intrigued, she curled her fingers over the chair's seat, gripping the edge on either side of her thighs. Her body leaned forward as if she were anchored only by her hold on the chair. "Are you selling the sculpture I saw in the Lodge, the one of the running mustangs that hangs on the wall behind the registration desk? Because if so, you don't need an exhibit. I'm sure I could give you a list of collectors that would be anxious to bid in a private auction."

"No, that belongs to Zach and I think he wants to keep it."

Hazel eyes considered him for a moment. "You said 'originals,' plural. You found new pieces, didn't you?"

"Yes. Enough for a gallery showing, provided we can interest the right gallery," he confirmed.

"So let me see if I have this right." She lifted her hands to tick off conclusions. "You will allow me access to your mother's…" She paused. "Exactly what *do* I get to look at?"

"Family photos and some of Mom's journals."

"She left journals?" Excitement spiked in her voice and lit her eyes.

"She kept journals most of her life, from the time she was a little girl until the morning she died," Eli told her.

"That's wonderful!" Amanda exclaimed, her delighted smile blinding. She drew a deep breath and went back to counting off items on her fingers. "So I can have access to Melanie's journals and family photos. In return, all I have to do is ask my brother-in-law if he'll consent to a showing of her artwork?"

"And you'll have to sign a contract stipulating that you won't print anything about the family following her death."

Eli could almost see the swift calculations of her brain as she considered his caveat.

"Done." She held out her hand and Eli took it. Her palm and fingers were slim and soft, warm and female, enclosed in his.

"You won't be able to take the journals or photos from the ranch," he warned her. He steeled himself against the urge to tug her closer. The feel of her skin beneath his fingers tempted him nearly beyond reason. Barely two feet separated her body from his and he couldn't keep from wondering if the tender hollow at the base of her throat, framed by the collar of her blouse, was just as soft. Connected by their hands, he was swamped by the feminine, flowery scent she wore. With an effort, he yanked his thoughts back to the journals. "I'll bring them to the studio and clear a space for you to go over them. I have to be present while you're studying them, and you can't wander around the ranch."

"You're going to guard me while I'm on the Triple C?" A faint frown drew down her brows and anger sparked in her voice. "Are you afraid I'll steal something?"

"I'm being cautious. I don't know you, beyond the bio information I read on the *Artist* magazine's website. Until I know you well enough to decide if I can trust you, I'll keep an eye on you."

"Hmm." She glanced down at their clasped hands, apparently only just then realizing he still held her hand in his. She tugged and he released her. Could that be embarrassment in his eyes? "I suppose that's reasonable. But if you treat me like a potential thief after we know each other better, I'm not going to stay silent and meekly let you get away with it," she warned him firmly.

"Fair enough." He nodded in agreement, amused when she continued to frown at him, as if gauging the depth of his commitment.

"Very well. That's settled." She rose and walked into the bathroom, returning a second later with a cell phone. "I'll call Tom." Her eyes glowed with suppressed excitement as she tapped in a number. "You have no idea how interested he's going to be." She paused. "Tom? This is Amanda. Yes, I'm still in Montana." She listened for a moment before laughing. "Tell her Auntie Manda loves her, too." Another pause. "I have some news I think you'll find fascinating. I've just had a conversation with Eli Coulter. His family is interested in selling some of their mother's sculptures." She winced and held the phone away from her ear.

Eli clearly heard the male voice, although he couldn't make out the actual words.

"I take it you're interested?" Amanda spoke into the phone. "Very well. I'll tell him. And I'll get back to you as soon as I can."

She hung up and laid the small red phone on the tabletop.

"He's in. He has a lot of questions—like how soon you'll be ready, how many pieces will go on display and on sale, that sort of thing." She waved one slim hand. "He's very excited and wants to talk to you as soon as you've made any decisions about details."

"Good." Eli nodded and stood to stare down at her, studying her face. "You knew he'd agree, didn't you?"

"I thought he would," she admitted. "He's a big fan of your mother's work."

Eli wondered if he'd just been conned, but he couldn't deny he was relieved that the gallery and auction piece of the plan had been achieved so easily. And convincing Amanda to sign a contract agreeing to disclose nothing in her book about life on the Triple C following his mother's death was the best plan he could come up with to protect his family's privacy. All in all, he still liked the bargain they'd struck. "I should be able to tell him more in a few days, after I've chosen the pieces we want to sell."

"Are there a lot to choose from?" Amanda asked. When he didn't confirm or deny, curiosity filled her expression. "You might as well tell me. I'll find out from Tom."

"Not today," he told her calmly.

"You really aren't going to trust me until I prove myself, are you?" she shot back.

"No, ma'am." He looked at her. "I learned a long time ago it's best to be careful." He had a swift, sudden image of the swarm of reporters that had questioned, cajoled and then harassed him and his brothers after his mother died.

"You're an advocate of keeping your friends close and your enemies closer?"

"It's not a bad policy," he told her. "Especially if they're reporters."

"Tell me, Mr. Coulter," she said, narrowing her eyes over him. "Do you actually *have* any friends?"

"Yes, ma'am." He smiled with amusement. "I surely do."

"And did you put all of them through this—" she waved a hand in frustration "—this test, or whatever you call it?"

"Yeah, I did."

"Then I suppose the only thing that should surprise me is that you have friends at all."

He smiled and headed for the door. Pulling it open, he looked back at her. Her slim figure was taut with annoyance. She looked cute as hell.

"I should be ready to go to the studio around ten tomorrow morning, if you want to drive out and meet me at the house."

"I'll be there," she said tightly.

He nodded and closed the door, striding down the hallway and the flight of stairs to reach his truck and head back to the Triple C.

In Room 203, Amanda stood perfectly still for a long moment, frowning at the door panels.

Annoyance at Eli's blunt declaration that he didn't

trust her warred with elation that the Coulter family had consented to cooperate with her biography.

And I can read Melanie's journals, look at family photographs.

To Amanda's knowledge, this was the first time any of the Coulters, including their deceased father, Joseph, had granted access to any of Melanie Coulter's personal possessions.

She spun in a circle, delight at the huge breakthrough zinging through her veins. Then she caught up her cell phone and quickly tapped in a number.

"Lindsey, I have the most fabulous news," she said, her voice bubbling with excitement when her sister answered. "The Coulter family is going to give me exclusive access to Melanie Coulter's journals and family photos."

"Wow! Congratulations," Lindsey said with pleased surprise. "I thought her sons turned you down and practically tossed you off the ranch? How did you convince them to cooperate?"

"Eli Coulter wants to auction off some of his mother's sculptures, and you, brilliant sister of mine, happen to be married to the owner of the best art gallery in New York!"

"Seriously?" Lindsey said. "Well, I always knew Tom was the best at everything," she added with a laugh. "But I didn't know about the Coulter sculptures. How marvelous is that?"

"It's more than I dared hope for." Amanda laughed, unable to keep her delight contained. "Oh, Lindsey, I think this may give me the personal touch I so badly wanted for the book."

"Congratulation, sis," Lindsey said fondly. "I couldn't be more pleased and happy for you."

"There is one small concern," Amanda told her. "It's apparent the Coulters don't trust reporters or writers."

"But that's not unusual, right? I thought not being trusted was something you've grown used to while reporting?"

"Oh, it is," Amanda agreed. "Of course it is. I wish Eli wasn't so cynical about reporters, though."

"Really?" Lindsey said with obvious surprise. Then she made a small hum of understanding. "You're interested in him."

"No, of course not," Amanda denied instantly.

"Yes, you are," Lindsey said with conviction. "I've never heard that note in your voice before when you were talking about a less-than-friendly interview."

"What note?" Amanda asked defensively.

"That wistful longing." Lindsey laughed with delight. "Tell me about Eli—would I like him?"

"Of course you'd like him," Amanda answered quickly before she groaned aloud. "You tricked me. Stop that. My only interest in Eli is that he's willing to let me see his mother's journals and photos. And now that I think about it," she went on, "I'm sure he'll stop worrying once he gets to know me."

"Of course he will," Lindsey said stoutly. "And if he doesn't, you only have to be there long enough to finish your research. Then you can come home and get on with the actual writing of the book. Hang in there."

"Words to live by," Amanda said with a laugh. "You're right, of course."

After chatting a few more moments about their parents and the latest antics of Lindsey's one-year-old daughter, Emma, Amanda said goodbye.

She hoped Lindsey was right about Eli getting past his distrust. If not, the next few weeks might prove to be uncomfortable on a daily basis.

Too bad he's decided I can't be trusted, she thought with a sigh, *because he's the most interesting man I've ever met.*

Determined to deal with the breath-stealing attraction, which apparently was one-sided, Amanda slipped into her pumps, caught up her purse and headed out for her lunch appointment.

She would focus on the amazing piece of luck that allowed her access to Melanie Coulter's journals and photos.

She would not waste one moment wishing Eli considered her more than a means to auctioning Melanie's artwork in New York.

Chapter Five

Amanda turned off the highway and drove beneath the iron arch of the Coulter Cattle Company sign just before 10:00 a.m. the next morning. A plume of dust rose behind her rented car as she drove down the gravel ranch road. The bridge rattled beneath her wheels as she crossed the creek before braking to a stop, parking just outside the ranch house fence.

Before she could step out, the house door opened and Eli appeared. He walked toward her with a loose, easy stride that riveted her attention on his long legs. Faded jeans hugged his thighs and hips and were nearly white from wear in interesting places. A black T-shirt with a Spanish logo left his tanned arms bare, and his black cowboy boots were covered with dust.

She was glad the dark lenses of her sunglasses hid her eyes as she rolled down the window to look up at him.

"Good morning." Her voice was throatier than normal but she refused to acknowledge his effect on her.

"Morning," he replied, bending slightly to look at her. The brim of his gray Stetson shaded his face and mirrored sunglasses concealed his eyes. "We'll drive down to the studio. Give me a minute and you can follow me." If her appearance at the ranch had any effect on him, he certainly didn't show it.

She nodded. "All right."

He turned and strode to an older-model pickup. Moments later Amanda followed the truck as Eli drove past the barn.

There was a lot of activity at the corral attached to the barn. Several people, both men and women, perched on the corral poles, and inside, dust rose from several horses that milled around a center post.

Amanda wished she had time to stop and see what they were doing, but the truck ahead of her didn't slow or pause, so she dutifully followed. Eli's pickup followed the graveled lane away from the barn, passing a picturesque log cabin and continuing on until he slowed further before turning into a shady drive.

She pulled her car alongside his truck, excitement shivering and tightening her nerves as she realized that the low building with its lawn sloping down to the creek bank must be where Melanie Coulter had worked.

She pushed open her door, grabbed her laptop and purse, and left the car to join Eli at the back of his truck.

The long muscles of his back flexed as he leaned into the truck bed and lifted out two medium-size boxes.

"I haven't been down here to set up a table for you yet," he said as he led the way up the shallow steps and onto the porch. "But it won't take more than a few minutes." The unlocked door gave way under his hand and he pushed the door inward, stepping back to wave her ahead of him.

She was vividly aware of him as she moved past him, and she cast a quick glance sideways. He was watching her and she caught her breath at the clear impatience mixed with a distinctly male interest in his green eyes. Then she looked away, determined to ignore the heightened tension between them as she crossed the threshold.

The long room was quiet, almost hushed, and Amanda felt as if she were entering a museum. Her gaze lingered over the workbench, with tools hung on the wall above, before finding the huge rock fireplace that took up most of the far wall.

She jumped as Eli brushed past her to set the two boxes he carried down on the workbench.

"This should be enough space for you to get started." He lifted a folding table from a rack halfway down the room and returned to the center. He unfolded the legs, locked them into place and set the table down before glancing up. "Come in," he told her with a faint frown.

She realized she'd been standing just inside the doorway, studying the room with intent fascination while purposely avoiding Eli's gaze.

"Sorry." She walked forward as he collected the two boxes from the workbench and set them on the table, then turned back to snag an office chair and roll it to the table.

"No problem." He glanced around the room. "Why don't you put your things down and I'll give you the five-cent tour? Not that there's much to see," he added as she complied. "Dad built the studio for Mom right after they were married." He waved a hand at the workbench that ran the length of one wall. "She did all her work here." He moved forward, Amanda trailing after him. "The building is self-contained. She used the little kitchen for making coffee mostly."

Amanda hurried to keep up with his long strides as he walked the length of the long room.

"The bathroom's here...."

Careful to leave distance between them, she peered past him, into a small but complete facility with a shower stall.

"And this is a storage room...."

Again, he held the door open and she looked past him to see a small room lined with shelving where packing boxes and bubble wrap sat side by side with neat stacks of office supplies. He stood close enough that she could smell his rugged, masculine scent. *Focus,* she warned herself.

"She used to take naps on the sofa or sit there to draw designs." He pointed to the floral blue-and-white sofa with a high back and fat, rolled arms that stood facing French doors, looking out on a deck and the creek beyond. "Not this sofa. The mice wrecked the old one and we replaced it." He paused, hands on hips, and surveyed the space. "That's about it." He walked back to the table where she'd left her purse and laptop. "Until we get to know each other better, you'll need to leave your purse and laptop case on the bench with me. You'll find paper, pens and pencils in one of the boxes for notes."

Anger rose, swift and sure, quickly tamping down the attraction she had been fighting. "I assume this is part of your 'don't trust reporters until you've tested them' policy?"

"That's right." His voice was brusque, but his green eyes were watchful, stormy with emotion.

Amanda considered telling him exactly how outrageous she thought he was being but decided against it. She'd had to leave her purse and briefcase with security when interviewing prisoners for an article on art theft, but being subjected to those steps here was infuriating. However, in light of what he'd told her about his negative experience with reporters when he was a child, newly traumatized by his mother's tragic death and his later interactions as an adult, she decided perhaps he had a right to distrust the press. "I'll expect an apology in a week or two," she told him firmly, her gaze holding his without flinching.

He nodded briefly. "If things pan out, you'll get one." He pointed at the boxes. "One of the boxes has journals. The other contains a collection of family photos."

He opened the boxes, then turned to look at her, folding his arms across his chest.

For a moment, Amanda simply stared back at him. He clearly expected her to say something but she had no idea what to reply. So she picked up her purse and laptop case, walked to the workbench to set them down, and turned on her heel to return to the table.

"If it's all right with you, I'll begin." She couldn't keep the frosty annoyance from bleeding into her voice and couldn't bring herself to care. If he didn't like it, tough, she thought.

His eyes darkened, and for a moment, Amanda thought he was going to say something important and every nerve in her body tightened. But then he shrugged and his expression was unreadable once more.

"Fine by me." He jerked his thumb in the direction

of the kitchenette. "I'll put some coffee on. It's done when the machine beeps. Feel free to help yourself."

"Thanks." She waited until he turned away, tension vibrating between them before she sat and peered into the open boxes, torn as to which to choose first. Opting for a journal, she lifted out a spiral-bound notebook. The first page was covered in block letters scrawled in a childish hand. Amanda calculated quickly and realized that based on the date scribbled at the top of the page, Melanie must have been ten years old when she wrote the words.

Delighted, she bent over the notebook and began to read. Quickly becoming absorbed in the comments, she determinedly ignored Eli when he went outside to his truck and returned with a box.

Silence filled the room, broken only by the soft rustle of turning pages and the faint sound of cloth rubbing over metal.

"Oh, my." Amanda's soft gasp was reverent, filled with awe.

"What is it?" Eli was certain he'd checked the notebooks for loose papers or any personal comments his mother would have wanted kept private. The journals he'd given Amanda were written when Melanie was a young girl and he didn't think there could possibly be anything controversial or shocking in them. Nevertheless, he left his stool at the workbench to join her and look over Amanda's shoulder.

"Your mother sketched in her journals, too," Amanda said. The tip of her index finger carefully traced the decisive black ink strokes of an eagle in flight that filled the page. The simple sketch conveyed the fierceness of the raptor and his joy at the wind that lifted his wings as he soared. "Look how amazingly good she was, even as a child."

Relief washed over Eli. He inspected the sketch, his trained eye seeing the mistakes while acknowledging the obvious talent. "She was born with a gift," he agreed.

Amanda half turned in her chair to look up at him. "Did you spend a lot of time here in the studio with your mother? Was she your first art teacher?"

Eli didn't answer for a moment. Her face was lit with bright-eyed interest and he could discern no sign that she was probing for information. Still, he reminded himself, he didn't know her well enough to judge whether she was being deceptive. His gaze left hers to move over the long room, lingering on the tools his mother had used, her favorite stool at the workbench, and her tarnished sculpture he was currently cleaning.

"I spent more time here with mom than my brothers did. She was always happy to have us, although we must have interrupted her work. She kept a big box of toys and art supplies for us to play with when we were in here."

"And did you know early on that you would be an artist?" Amanda asked. She waved a hand at the journal, open to the sketch of the eagle. "Like your mother, I mean. Clearly, she was already working when she was quite young."

Eli glanced from the open journal to Amanda's face. "Are you asking as a reporter? Or as an interested fan?"

His question wiped the warm interest from her expression. Her full lips firmed, tightening. "I'm writing a biography about your mother, Eli. I don't have to include your story. Unless, of course, you want me to," she added coolly.

"Hell, no," he said with feeling.

She studied him for a moment, her hazel eyes assessing behind the narrow black frames of her glasses. "I don't think I've ever met an artist who's been quite as adamant about avoiding publicity as you apparently are. Don't you want to reach a larger audience for your work?"

"Not if it means giving up my privacy," he answered without hesitation. "I wouldn't mind being rich but I don't want to be famous."

"Why not?" She leaned back in her chair, crossing slim arms over her chest. The move drew her white knit top tighter over her chest, outlining the full swell of her breasts. "I thought every artist wanted to be famous."

"Not me." Eli shook his head.

"So you don't want a wider fan base that loves your work?" she asked skeptically.

"Ah, now that's a whole other subject," he corrected her. "I'm always glad to know someone appreciates my work. But that's not the same as being famous myself."

She frowned and sat up straighter, moving forward to the edge of her chair and spreading her hands in a gesture that reflected her confusion. "Aren't we talking about one and the same thing?"

"No, we're not. People can enjoy my work without ever meeting me, or knowing my name and what I look like. Appreciating a piece of art has nothing to do with whether the viewer appreciates the personality of the artist."

She pursed her lips, narrowing her eyes at him. "Don't tell me you're one of those reclusive hermit who refuses to appear at gallery showings," she said suspiciously.

He grinned. She reminded him of a cute little hen, feathers ruffled and ready to attack, at least verbally, if he confirmed her suspicions.

"No," he reassured her. "I attend gallery openings. And I chat with all the patrons. I'm charming to the little gray-haired ladies and I ignore the women who try to get too touchy-feely after they've finished their third glass of wine. I draw the line at getting patted on the butt, though," he told her solemnly. "And I never sleep with anyone just because they're willing to pay me an exorbitant amount of money for one of my sculptures. Frankly, it feels too much like prostitution."

Eli held back a laugh when Amanda's eyes widened at his last sentence.

"If a man does that to a woman," she said with a frown, "it's called sexual harassment."

"It is," he agreed. "But in my experience, women with a little too much wine in their system aren't able to make that connection."

"You shouldn't have to put up with that kind of treatment," she said firmly.

"I agree. That's why I don't let it happen twice. At least not with the same semi-inebriated woman," he added.

"I've been to lots of gallery exhibit openings," she told him, "and while I noticed artists being hit on by the opposite sex, I never thought anyone seemed upset by the attention."

Eli shrugged. "Some aren't. I have friends who consider the number of women willing to bed the most artists one of the perks of the job."

"But you're not one of them." It wasn't a question.

"No," Eli said. "I'm definitely not one of them. I prefer my women sober." He studied her, the gleam of her hair, the intelligence in the hazel eyes that watched him, the plump curve of her bottom lip and the swell of breasts beneath the modest white knit top. "And if I'm interested, I like to make the first move."

A faint flush colored her cheeks as she stared at him, but she didn't lower her lashes or look away. "So, you prefer to be the one with your hand on a strange woman's butt rather than the other way around?"

He chuckled. "I hope I'd have a little more finesse with a stranger, but yes, that's the general idea."

Her lips curved in an answering smile. "You're an old-fashioned man, Mr. Coulter. I never would have guessed."

"I suppose I am in some ways. Certainly when it comes to courting a woman."

Her smile brimmed with delight; her eyes filled with wicked amusement. "And the term 'courting a woman' is totally old-school. Are you a romantic, too?"

"Hell, no." He shook his head, affronted. "I haven't got a romantic bone in my body."

"No?" She tilted her head a bit to the side, the end of her ponytail swinging to brush her shoulder. "You sound like a romantic kind of guy."

"I'm old-fashioned enough to prefer being the pursuer in a relationship," he corrected her. "That doesn't make me a romantic."

She pursed her lips consideringly. "That's what it sounds like to me," she said, clearly not convinced.

"I don't believe in hearts and flowers, living happily

ever after and wedding bells," he told her. "Ergo, I'm not romantic."

"So you're radically different from your brothers, then?"

Eli almost growled, all amusement fleeing as he frowned. "I didn't think so six months ago. But apparently there's something about returning to Montana that spun them around one hundred eighty degrees." He shrugged. "Or it's the women. I have to admit, Mariah and Cynthia seem to fit Cade and Zach."

"And you never thought that would happen?"

Her comment was too insightful, too dead on target to be comfortable. His muscles twitched and his gut clenched, but since Amanda's expression didn't change, he was fairly sure she didn't notice.

"No, I didn't. I guess I never thought any of us would find partners, let alone get married," he told her.

"Maybe you and Brodie won't," she pointed out.

"I'd say that's a safe bet in any poker game," he responded with conviction.

"Well, then..." She spread her hands wide and shrugged. "That settles that." Was it Eli's imagination or did she suddenly seem annoyed?

Eli wasn't sure how they'd drifted into the quagmire of discussing whether or not he and Brodie would marry, but he was damn sure he was glad to be done with the subject. He turned and walked to the kitchenette. "Want some coffee?" he asked over his shoulder as he took two mugs out of the cabinet.

"Yes, please."

Eli delivered a mug of coffee to Amanda, nodded a silent acceptance of her thanks and returned to the stool at the workbench. For the next hour, there was little conversation as she seemed to concentrate on the journals, occasionally jotting notes on a tablet. Although he was aware of every move Amanda made, no matter how slight, Eli forced himself to focus on the meticulous removal of tarnish from the sculpture. He used soft towels and polish, choosing a time-tested method rather than a battery-operated or electric buffer. Cleaning the pieces would take longer this way, but he wouldn't trust his mother's work to anything less.

His cell phone rang just before one o'clock. He glanced at his watch, nodding as he listened to Cade's request. "No problem. I'll be right there."

"We'll have to cut today's session short," he told Amanda when he hung up. He stood and settled the sculpture back into the padded box. "Some of our cattle are out and Cade needs my help. I'll be mending fence this afternoon."

She looked up, closing the notebook. "Of course." She tucked Melanie's journal back into the cardboard box. "I assume I can take my notes with me? I'd like to transcribe them into my laptop file tonight."

"Sure." Eli couldn't think of any reason to refuse her request.

"Thank you." She walked to the workbench, tucked her tablet into a side pocket of her laptop bag and picked up both it and her purse.

Eli stepped back to wave her ahead of him. The subtle feminine scent of her perfume teased him as she brushed past, and his muscles tightened in reaction. Jaw set, he followed her to the exit, holding the door open, the box tucked under his arm.

She stepped out onto the porch, and he joined her,

pausing to lock the door before walking behind her down the sidewalk.

She pulled open her car door and paused to look back at him. "Should I meet you here tomorrow?" Her voice was even; her gaze calm behind her glasses.

Clearly, he thought, she didn't share the tension that slammed him every time she was near.

"It's probably better if you stop at the house," he told her. "If I'm not there, try the barns. I'm working with Cade and Zach in the south pasture in the morning but I should be back by ten."

"All right. See you tomorrow, then." She slid into the car and moments later lifted a hand in farewell as she drove away.

Eli leaned against the tailgate of his truck and watched dust rise up from behind her car until it disappeared over the rise of the hill. Why did he suddenly feel a sense of loss?

Sharing the studio with the pretty writer had left him tense and irritable. Amanda Blake wasn't a woman who chattered nonstop, nor had she asked a lot of annoying questions. Except for the moments when she'd shown him the eagle sketch in his mother's journal, she'd focused on reading and taking notes, pretty much ignoring him. Despite that, he'd been unable to get much done during their few hours in the studio. He had long hours of painstaking tarnish removal to complete before moving his mother's sculptures to New York for the auction. If Amanda continued to be a distraction, he wouldn't be able to estimate the amount of time needed to prepare for the showing with the gallery. And the sooner he could confirm a date for the auction, the closer he would be to bringing in income to pay off the tax debt hovering over the Triple C.

That couldn't happen fast enough, he thought. The sooner the taxes were paid, the better. Then they could focus on making the ranch a thriving enterprise again.

All he had to do was turn off his attraction to Amanda Blake for a few hours a day. They'd made a good bargain: she got what she wanted with exclusive access to his mother's journals and photos, while he received her assistance in locking in her brother-in-law's gallery for the auction.

She doesn't have to know how badly I wanted her signature on the contract clause saying she couldn't publish any comments about the family after Mom died, he thought.

Now all he had to do was remember she was off-limits for anything beyond business.

Just because something about her made his body switch into "me Tarzan, you Jane" mode and demanded he get closer, intimately closer, didn't mean he had to act on it.

He'd known lots of women he'd been attracted to but never slept with. Amanda would have to stay on that list. .

He could do this.

He ignored the snicker of amusement from his conscience that whispered Amanda was different. He spent the rest of the afternoon working nonstop, digging fence post holes, stringing wire and chasing cattle that stubbornly resisted being returned to their own side of the fence line. He purposely tried to physically wear himself out. But when he fell into bed that night, he dreamed of Amanda's hazel eyes sparkling with amusement behind the narrow black frames of her glasses and the plump, lush curve of her mouth.

Chapter Six

Amanda settled into a routine over the next week. She rose early, went jogging and stopped at the café for breakfast, often spending a few moments exchanging pleasantries with Mariah. Then she walked back to the hotel to shower, dress and head out to the Triple C. At the ranch, Eli met her outside his house and she followed his truck as they drove to the studio. Once inside, she settled at the table to read journals, study photos and make notes, while Eli painstakingly cleaned tarnish from one or another of his mother's sculptures. She tried valiantly to ignore the way Eli made her feel. There was no point in it. He'd made it clear he wasn't interested in a relationship with anyone, much less a reporter he didn't trust.

When she'd read all the journals and looked at all the photos in the first two boxes, Eli brought her more. Amanda loved reading the journals. Melanie Coulter had not only been a brilliant artist, but she'd had an amazing ability to make scenes come alive in her diaries, with her vivid, descriptive phrases.

On Tuesday morning Amanda gathered her courage and turned in her chair to look at Eli. His boot heels were hooked over the rungs of the stool; his head bent as he focused on a two-foot sculpture of an eagle, wings lifted in flight, on the workbench in front of him.

"Eli?"

He turned his head sideways and looked her, his eyes losing their distracted haze to focus intently on her. "Yes?"

"Your mother was a wonderful writer. Even as a young child, she was able to articulate an amazing insight into the world around her and how that translated into her need to create images." Amanda lifted the notebook she held, opening to a page with an ink sketch of a horse. "It's fascinating to see that awareness of the world develop, and repeat itself at more depth, in her journals from year to year."

"I felt the same when I read them," he told her. "She told me once that she knew I'd be a successful artist someday because my drawings reminded her of her own at that age."

"How old were you when she said that?" Amanda asked, curious.

"Six or seven, I think. I don't remember precisely." Eli looked past her, out the glass doors. "It was summer and we were sitting on the deck. She had her sketchbook and I had mine—we were drawing the horses in the pasture across the creek. When I showed her my sketch, she hugged me, told me that someday I'd be a famous artist, just like her." His eyes were distant, the lines of his mouth softened with affection.

"She was a great mom, wasn't she?" Amanda said, touched by the obvious love he felt for his mother.

"The best." Eli gestured at the long worktable. "I spent hours in here with her, working next to her. I realized after I was older that she must have often put her own work on hold to answer my questions and show me how to work silver."

With sudden clarity, the enormity of the loss Eli had endured when his mother died struck Amanda anew. Not only had he lost his mother, but he'd lost the mentor guiding his earliest artistic efforts. Before she could speak, Eli shook his head as if to clear it. When his gaze met hers, he was once again focused and intent, the very intimate moment between them gone.

"She was an amazing woman in all respects," he told her. "I hope your book will reflect that."

"When I came to Montana, I was a huge fan of your mother's work. Everything I've learned since I've been here has made me an even greater admirer of the person she was," Amanda told him. She paused to draw a breath. "I would very much like to quote some passages from her journals and use some of her sketches as illustrations in my book."

Eli's eyes narrowed over her, a faint frown pleating two lines between his dark eyebrows. "How many?" he asked.

"Perhaps five to ten." She held her breath, hardly daring to hope.

He considered her, his face inscrutable. "I'll think about it and let you know in a day or two," he said at last.

"Great. I appreciate it." It wasn't a yes, but it was better than an outright refusal, she thought. She'd count that as a success.

"That reminds me…" Eli wiped his hands on a black-smudged towel and reached into the padded box he carried the sculptures in. He took out a large manila envelope and removed a thin sheaf of papers. "The attorney drew up the contract that sets out the details of our agreement." He stood and, in two strides, reached her to hold out the documents. "There are two originals, one for you, one for me. I've already signed off on them."

Amanda took the papers from him and quickly glanced through them. "They seem fairly straightforward," she commented, quickly signing on the line above her typed name. "I assume I don't need to do anything with my original?" she asked, leaving her chair to place one set of the documents on the workbench's smooth surface, next to the sculpture. "Other than tucking it into a file in my office?"

"I don't believe so," he told her. "But I'll ask the attorney, if you want me to."

"I'd appreciate it." Her hazel gaze met his, curiosity on her expressive face. "I don't suppose you'd be willing to tell me why you insisted my book doesn't include comments on your family after the date of your mother's death?"

"No, I don't suppose I would," he told her.

She contemplated him for a moment, studying his face. Apparently, his expression was as unreadable as he'd hoped, because she sighed with disappointment.

"I was afraid you'd say that." Her gaze moved to the eagle sculpture. "This reminds me of your mother's sketch in the first journal I read."

Eli was relieved to move on to another subject. He, too, looked at the partially cleaned sculpture. "Yes, it does. Mom loved eagles and mustangs. She sculpted them many times. There are at least half a dozen of them that I plan to sell."

"My brother-in-law is going to love you," she commented absently, still focused on the sleek, flowing lines of the eagle in flight.

"Really? Why?" Eli studied her face as she studied the sculpture.

"Because he's a huge fan of your mother's work," she told him, her gaze returning to meet his. "And of yours, as well. In fact, he told me he'd love to include some pieces of yours in your mother's exhibit. Whether or not you choose to make them part of the auction is up to you, of course."

"I've been out of the country for a year," he told her. "I don't have a collection at the moment."

"I know he'll be sorry to hear that," she said. "I'm sure he'll want to discuss a future showing of your work whenever you're ready."

"Good to know," he said. "Thanks for telling me."

"You're welcome." Her smile flashed, quick and enchanting. "Now, I'd better get back to work and let you get back to yours."

She returned to her seat, and for the next hour, the only sounds in the quiet studio were the rustle of pages turning and the soft sound of cloth rubbing against metal.

The near silence held until once again, Eli's phone rang.

"Yeah? Hey, Mariah."

Amanda brushed her hair back behind her ear and

pretended not to eavesdrop. Given that Eli was sitting only a few feet away, however, it was impossible not to hear his side of the conversation.

"Sure, I'll ask her." He paused. "Mariah's at the Lodge with Cynthia. She wants to know if we want to have lunch with them."

"I'd love to," she said, startled, after a moment spent trying to discern from his expression whether he wanted her to say yes or refuse. Since she couldn't tell how he felt about the invitation, she decided to go with her first reaction.

He merely nodded and lifted the phone to his ear. "She says yes. See you in a few minutes." He snapped the phone closed and shoved it into his pocket, standing. "It's not far to the Lodge, so I thought we'd walk. Okay with you?"

"Yes, absolutely." Amanda joined him, stepping outside when he held the door open and waiting while he locked it behind them. His long legs quickly moved him ahead of her, and she hurried to keep up until he glanced sideways and purposely slowed his strides.

They left the studio driveway and turned right along the gravel lane. The sun was nearly straight overhead and Amanda was thankful she'd remembered to take her sunglasses from her purse and slide them on her nose before leaving the studio. The road followed the bend of the creek and wound to the left, the bungalow on the creek bank dropping out of sight behind them while the Lodge loomed just ahead.

"You need a hat."

"I beg your pardon?" Amanda asked, tearing herself away from the view of the beautiful two-story log building with its wide porches. Eli wore mirrored sunglasses beneath the brim of his gray Stetson and she couldn't see his eyes. But she could feel him looking at her.

"I said you should be wearing a hat," he repeated. He frowned and laid his palm on the crown of her head. He barely touched her before the weight of his palm was gone. "The sun's hot, especially at midday."

"I have a baseball cap I use when I run in the morning," she told him, still tingling from the brief touch of his hand against her hair. "I suppose I could start wearing it during the day, too, when I'm outside."

He shrugged. "A cap's better than nothing, but a Stetson crown and brim give you more protection. I have one in the closet that I wore when I was about twelve. It might be small enough for you. I'll check at the house."

"Thank you." Bemused, she stared at him, but he was already facing forward again. Just when she'd decided he barely tolerated her for the sake of their bargain, he said or did something nice and knocked her off balance. *Who are you, Eli Coulter?*

They neared the Lodge and Eli veered to the left on a walkway that skirted the wide green lawn edged with flower beds and tall old maple trees. The overhanging branches shaded the path and their protection immediately gave Amanda relief from the sun's hot rays. They walked past a low hedge that divided the lawn from a neat kitchen garden with arrow-straight lines of mulch separating rows of lush green plants.

"What a beautiful garden," Amanda commented.

"That's Jane's work," Eli told her. "She's the chef at the Lodge. Both she and Cynthia are advocates of organic food served as fresh as possible. I'm not a gardener, but given how good the meals are here, I have to assume they're right."

Amanda remembered very clearly how delicious the food had been at the Lodge's open house and suspected the women were on the right track.

The path ended at a set of shallow, wide steps that led up onto the deck at the back of the Lodge, and Eli ushered her through a door that opened directly into the big kitchen.

A slim woman wearing a white chef's jacket and slacks stood at the big commercial range with her back to the room, stirring something in a big stockpot. Cynthia perched on a tall stool at the counter, knees crossed, one slim foot swinging in time to the classic rock music coming from a radio in the far corner. As they entered, Mariah bumped the refrigerator door closed with her hip, a pitcher of iced tea in one hand, the other balancing a huge bowl of salad. She looked up as she walked toward the island counter, a smile lighting her face when she saw Eli and Amanda.

"Hi, there." Mariah's cheerful greeting was echoed by Cynthia, who turned at her words.

"I hope you're hungry," Cynthia said. "We're having salad and Jane's classic stir-fry. She had porterhouse steak on the menu last night and we get the leftovers."

"Sounds good to me," Eli drawled. He pulled out a stool and seated Amanda. "Amanda, I don't know if you've met Cynthia and Jane. Cynthia is Zach's fiancée and also manager of the Lodge. Jane is the Lodge chef and rules the kitchen. Jane, Cynthia, this is Amanda Blake."

"Hello." Amanda had seen the stunningly beautiful Cynthia with Zach from across the lobby at the Lodge's grand opening but they hadn't been properly introduced. She hadn't seen Jane before, neither here on the ranch nor in Indian Springs, but the slim redhead's quiet smile as she looked over her shoulder to nod a welcome reassured Amanda.

"It's very nice to meet you." Cynthia's expression was warm and friendly as she openly studied Amanda. "I understand you're writing a book about Zach's mother?"

"Yes, I am." Before she could say anything more, Jane left the stove to slide a large steaming bowl of vegetables with chunks of meat in broth onto the countertop. It smelled heavenly, reminding Amanda she hadn't eaten since breakfast at the café in Indian Springs six hours earlier.

Mariah set a bowl of fluffy white rice on the countertop and took her seat. "I'm starving," she announced. "You're joining us, aren't you, Jane?"

"Yes, I'm just waiting for Harley. Matty's dropping him off for lunch."

Amanda belatedly noticed that there were six places set at the counter. Before she had time to do more than wonder who Harley was, the back door opened and a little boy dashed into the kitchen.

"Mama, guess what?" His face radiated excitement. A shock of tousled reddish-brown hair fell over his forehead and below eyebrows that were the same shade of brown, his bright blue eyes gleamed with delight. A light dusting of freckles highlighted the bridge of his short, straight nose in a face tanned golden-brown by the summer sun.

"Harley, stop running." Jane calmly intercepted him and steered him to the sink. "Where have you been? I expected you ten minutes ago."

"I stopped by the barn to see the puppies." His

words were muffled as Jane ran a damp washcloth over his face.

"Wash your hands," his mother instructed, turning on the faucet. "So they were born? I hadn't heard."

"Yes, they were borned." The little boy scrubbed his hands with reckless disregard for splattering water, rinsed and accepted the towel Jane held out. "And they're so little, Mama."

"I'm sure they are." Jane took his hand and drew him with her to the counter.

Eli stood and, without a word, lifted the little boy up onto the tall stool next to him while his mother settled on the one just beyond.

"Thanks, Mr. Eli." Harley flashed him a grin.

"You're welcome, Harley," Eli answered gravely.

The interaction between the little boy and Eli charmed Amanda. She couldn't help noticing how comfortable Harley clearly was with Eli. And how easily Eli dealt with the boy. She wondered fleetingly if he'd had practice with his own child, but none of her research on the Coulter family indicated that any of the brothers had children.

Apparently, Eli and his brothers liked children, however. She knew from earlier conversations with people in Indian Springs that they'd hired John and Matty Arnold some months earlier. The couple lived in a small house on the property and John was employed as a ranch hand, while Matty provided day care for Harley while Jane worked. The ranching community soundly approved of the Coulters creating a solution that allowed single parent Jane Howard to work as the Lodge chef.

"So, Harley, Belle had her babies?" Cynthia asked.

"Yes. She had eight." He held up two hands, fingers

splayed, visibly counting his digits and folding down the thumb and two fingers of his left hand.

"One more, little guy," Eli said quietly, nodding in approval when Harley laboriously unbent his little finger and proudly waved his hands.

"How many boys and how many girls?" Mariah asked, spooning rice onto her plate and passing the bowl to Cynthia on her left.

"John says four are boys and four are girls." Harley's face split into a wide grin. "And he said one of them can be mine if I promise to take care of it."

Amanda caught Jane's quick, exasperated amusement as her gaze flashed to meet Cynthia's.

"Oh, he did, did he?" Jane said mildly, no trace of negativity in her voice as she spoke to her son. "Did you tell him we can't have a puppy at the Lodge?"

"But, Mama," Harley pleaded. "I'd keep him in my room all the time, honest."

"But our apartment is right off the kitchen," she reminded him. "I'm not sure the Department of Health regulations would allow a dog here." She exchanged another long-suffering glance with Cynthia. "Even if Cynthia and Zach approved of it," she added.

Harley's face fell. "You'd let me have a puppy, wouldn't you, Cynthia?"

"I think that's something your mom and I—and Zach—would have to discuss, Harley." Cynthia's face was solemn but her eyes twinkled.

"In any event, the puppies have just been born," Jane reminded him calmly. "It's going to be quite a while before they're old enough to leave their mother. So we have some time to think about this. Meanwhile, you need to eat your lunch."

"Okay." The little boy's mouth drooped for a moment before he looked up, his expression hopeful once more. "When Miss Matty comes to get me, can I go see the puppies again before we go back to her house?"

"Only if Matty has time to stop at the barn with you," his mother said. "And if you eat all of your lunch."

"'Kay."

Bowls of rice, stir-fry, and salad had passed around the counter and plates had been filled during Harley's conversation. While Jane's son enthusiastically applied himself to emptying his plate, Amanda listened without comment while the four other adults discussed the up-coming weekend. The Lodge's guest rooms were filled to capacity and Cynthia had scheduled entertainment that included an outdoor barbecue on Saturday night, complete with a small local western band and dancing under the stars.

Amanda savored every bite of the delicious food as Cynthia told Eli about the carpenter she'd hired to build a wooden platform for the guests to dance on.

"He hasn't checked in and I haven't been able to reach him at the phone number he gave me." Cynthia frowned, worry pleating two vertical lines between her eyebrows. "Which makes me nervous about whether he's actually going to show up."

"Kenny hasn't been in the café for at least a week," Mariah told her. "And he usually eats lunch there every Tuesday and Thursday."

"Is Kenny Roberts the man you're talking about?" Amanda asked, hesitant to offer information unless it was needed.

"Yes, he is. Do you know him? Have you seen him recently?" Cynthia looked hopeful.

The Reader Service—Here's how it works:

If offer card is missing write to: The Reader Service, P.O. Box 1867, Buffalo, NY 14240-1867 or visit us at www.ReaderService.com.

NO POSTAGE
NECESSARY
IF MAILED
IN THE
UNITED STATES

BUSINESS REPLY MAIL
FIRST-CLASS MAIL   PERMIT NO. 717   BUFFALO, NY

POSTAGE WILL BE PAID BY ADDRESSEE

THE READER SERVICE

PO BOX 1867

BUFFALO NY 14240-9952

Play the Lucky Hearts Game

and get...

2 FREE BOOKS and
2 FREE MYSTERY GIFTS...
YOURS TO KEEP!

yes! I have scratched off the gold card.
Please send me my *2 FREE BOOKS* and
2 FREE MYSTERY GIFTS (gifts are worth about $10).
I understand that I am under no obligation to purchase
any books as explained on the back of this card.

Scratch Here!
Then look below to see what your
cards get you...*2 Free Books
& 2 Free Mystery Gifts!*

235/335 HDL FJDE

FIRST NAME

LAST NAME

ADDRESS

APT.#

CITY

STATE/PROV.   ZIP/POSTAL CODE

Visit us online at
www.ReaderService.com

Twenty-one gets you
2 FREE BOOKS and
2 FREE MYSTERY GIFTS!

Twenty gets you
2 FREE BOOKS!

Nineteen gets you
1 FREE BOOK!

TRY AGAIN!

Offer limited to one per household and not applicable to series that subscriber is currently receiving.

Your Privacy—The Reader Service is committed to protecting your privacy. Our Privacy Policy is available online at www.ReaderService.com or upon request from the Reader Service. We make a portion of our mailing list available to reputable third parties that offer products we believe may interest you. If you prefer that we not exchange your name with third parties, or if you wish to clarify or modify your communication preferences, please visit us at www.ReaderService.com/consumerschoice or write to us at Reader Service Preference Service, P.O. Box 9062, Buffalo, NY 14269. Include your complete name and address.

▼ **DETACH AND MAIL CARD TODAY!** ▼

H-SE-11/11

"I'm afraid I don't know him, nor have I seen him," Amanda replied. "But I had lunch with his grandmother, who happens to be the librarian in Indian Springs. She told me he was visiting his cousin in Wyoming and was involved in a car accident. I believe his leg was broken. Mrs. Roberts was very concerned about him and was hoping she could drive down and visit him when we chatted a week ago."

Eli glanced sideways at her, his expression contemplative. "You're getting to know quite a few people in Indian Springs," he told her.

She shrugged noncommittally, not certain if he viewed her growing familiarity with the residents of Indian Springs as a good or bad thing.

"Well, I'm glad she is," Cynthia said firmly. "Otherwise, I wouldn't have known what happened to Kenny. And I might have wasted more time waiting for him to contact me. Now I know I have to make alternate plans."

Amanda hid a smile when Eli narrowed his eyes suspiciously.

"I'm busy, Cynthia."

"But all I want you to do is help Zach with the carpentry work," she told him.

"Does Zach know you've drafted him to build a platform by Saturday?" Eli asked, one eyebrow rising in disbelief.

"No, but I'm sure he'll agree when he knows the situation. Please, Eli," she wheedled.

"All right." Eli heaved a sigh. "But you owe me. And I'm talking major debt here. This could cost you free dinners at the Lodge for the next month, plus handing over half of any bakery goods Mariah brings home from the café."

"Fine." Cynthia grinned at him. "I'll pass the bill on to Zach. And Mariah," she added with a twinkle as Mariah frowned at her.

Amanda could have sworn he growled, but it was a halfhearted effort at best. After watching him with his future sisters-in-law, little Harley and Jane, she was beginning to doubt Eli Coulter was anywhere near as coldhearted and uncaring as he claimed to be.

"I owe you, too, Amanda." Cynthia's voice interrupted Amanda's musings. "If you hadn't told us what happened to Kenny, I would have had far less time to enlist alternative builders. Please join us on Saturday. I can promise you fabulous food because Jane's in charge of the barbecue, and also fabulous music, since the musicians are all local boys."

"It's lovely of you to invite me, Cynthia, but you don't owe me," Amanda protested. She was vividly aware of Eli seated beside her. She couldn't believe he would want her to spend time with his family. He'd been very specific about confining her presence to the studio, and even then only with him present. She was pretty sure socializing with his future sisters-in-law was not on his list of approved activities.

"Come on, Eli," Cynthia coaxed. "Tell her she has to come."

Amanda looked up at him through the shield of her lashes. She couldn't read anything in his enigmatic expression.

"Since I'll have to cancel our time at the studio for the next day or so in order to build your dance floor, I suppose it's only fair she get equal time at the barbecue," he said at last.

"Yea, it's settled. You're coming, Amanda."

"If you're sure you want me, I'm delighted to accept." Amanda didn't look at Eli; instead she smiled across the countertop at Cynthia.

"Do I get to come to the party, Mama?" Harley asked.

"I don't think so, kiddo," Jane told him. "It's an adult party and I have to work. But Matty can walk you down to the Lodge from her house so you can have barbecued beef for your dinner. Would you like that?"

"Yes." His prompt response was so enthusiastic, the adults all laughed.

A rap on the back door interrupted them and a young woman poked her head inside.

"Matty!" Harley jumped down off his stool and raced across the room to grab her hand. "Can we stop and see the puppies on our way to your house? Please?"

The dark-haired woman laughed. "Definitely, if your mom says it's okay."

"If you have time to let him visit the puppies, that would be great, Matty," Jane told her.

"Let's go!" Harley tugged at his nanny's hand, turning her toward the doorway. "Bye, Mama," he said over his shoulder.

"Bye, Harley. Be good," Jane called after the two.

Matty managed a quick wave goodbye before Harley urged her over the threshold and the door closed behind them.

Within moments, the adults departed, too, leaving Jane to get on with preparations for the dinner menu.

By two-thirty, Amanda was on her way back to Indian Springs. As she drove, she mulled over the interesting family dynamic she'd observed during lunch at the Lodge.

Eli treated Mariah, Cynthia and Jane with the easy, comfortable acceptance a man might show his sisters. Yet he'd grown up with only males in the house.

Amanda knew he'd been just nine years old when his mother died. Which would mean he'd spent most of his formative years in an all-male household. She wondered if his casual attitude toward his future sisters-in-law meant he truly was glad his family was expanding. Or could it be that he didn't plan to be around long enough for it to impact his life?

Chapter Seven

Since Eli had to help Zach build the outdoor platform for the Lodge's Saturday barbecue, Amanda didn't go to the Triple C for two days. Instead, she spent Wednesday and Thursday interviewing a small group of Indian Springs residents about their friendship with Melanie Coulter and writing several pages about their comments. It was becoming increasingly clear to Amanda that Melanie Coulter was as well loved for her friendship and good heart as she was for her contributions to the art world.

None of the people she interviewed were forthcoming about Melanie's husband, Joseph, however. In fact, they were all so reserved and vague in their responses that she was beginning to get the impression she was being stonewalled. Their evasions raised a red flag. Rather than being diverted, which she was fairly sure they intended, she wondered what they were trying to hide.

When she arrived at the Triple C on Friday morning, a strange pickup truck with a large horse trailer was parked near the barn. Mariah and Cynthia waved at her from their perches atop the corral fence.

Curious, Amanda left her car and walked across the ranch yard to join them.

"What's going on?" she asked, sensing a buzz of excitement. Cade, Zach and Eli stood next to the truck and horse trailer, talking to the driver. Eli glanced up when she joined the two women, his expression intent and focused as it swept over her before he returned his attention to his brothers. As always, Amanda shivered under the stroke of his gaze, as if he'd reached out and smoothed his hand over her sensitive, bare skin. How she wished she could tell if he was happy she'd arrived. He seemed to run so hot and cold with her.

"We're welcoming a new family member. Come join us," Cynthia invited, patting the section of peeled pole beside her.

Amanda climbed the worn poles and perched on the top one, next to Cynthia. "Who is it?" she asked, puzzled.

"Not who, exactly," Mariah said, leaning forward to smile at her. "Eli's friend in Spain gave him an Andalusian mare. We've been impatiently waiting to meet her and she's finally arrived."

"Oh, I see," Amanda said politely. She didn't really understand why the Coulters, who had several beautiful horses already, would be so excited about a new horse. Yet clearly, they'd all taken time out of their busy day to meet her. *But then,* she acknowledged with a mental shrug, *I'm not a horse person.*

The four men moved to the back of the trailer, and

Cade helped the driver unlatch and swing wide the rear gate. Eli stepped into the big six-horse transport, disappearing as he moved farther into the interior. Moments later he reappeared, leading a horse. The mare's glossy deep brown coat gleamed in the sunshine, her long black mane and tail thicker, coarser-looking than her sleek coat. Eli turned with her, letting her dance in a circle with him at the center, the lead taut between them.

Amanda caught her breath.

The mare's expressive eyes were liquid brown and intelligent as she took in her surroundings through the long strands of her forelock. Her tail nearly brushed the fetlocks of her back legs as she circled Eli, testing the air with flared nostrils.

The Coulters and Amanda were silent, spellbound by the beautiful horse. In the corral behind Amanda, however, Cade's black stallion had no such inhibitions. He bugled a welcome, making Amanda jump and clutch the pole beneath her to keep from falling.

The mare lifted her muzzle and nickered, answering Jiggs, and Eli laughed out loud.

"I think Jiggs likes her, Cade," he called.

"I don't blame him," Cade said dryly. "She's a beauty."

"She is that," Zach agreed. "You didn't lie when you said she was pretty, Eli."

"She and Jiggs will have beautiful babies," Mariah said. She leaned toward Amanda. "What do you think of the Triple C's new potential mama?"

"She's amazing," Amanda said with conviction. Fascinated, she couldn't take her eyes off the mare. Everything about the Spanish horse was stunningly beautiful, from the sweep of her luxurious black mane and tail to the quick movements of her small hooves and the shift of supple muscles beneath her glossy hide as she moved. She'd never seen a creature like that in New York.

"I think I'm in love," Cynthia said fervently.

Zach looked over his shoulder and grinned. "If you were saying that about anyone other than Shakira, I'd be jealous," he told her. "But since I'm feeling the same way about her, I completely understand."

Amanda silently agreed with them both.

"I'm going to take her into the barn and get her settled," Eli told them. "Thanks for delivering her, Jack."

"No problem." The transport driver waved as he headed for his truck cab.

Amanda barely noticed when the truck drove away with the empty trailer. All her attention was focused on Eli and the mare. He slowly reeled in the lead, easing the mare closer until she stood within touching distance. Ears pricked forward, she watched him with alert eyes as he held out his hand. She lowered her muzzle, sniffing, before she let out a huff and lipped his palm.

Eli crooned, talking to the mare in low tones. Amanda couldn't make out the words, but the horse visibly relaxed and eased closer. Then he stroked his hand down the arch of her neck, beneath the thick mane, and she bumped his shoulder with her muzzle.

"She's not nervous, Eli," Cade commented. "Did you handle her in Spain?"

Eli nodded, his voice quiet. "Lucan and I went riding most mornings and always spent an hour or two at the barns afterward, so she knows me. She's one of Lucan's favorites."

"That's why she doesn't seem the least bit frightened," Mariah said softly. "She and Eli are old friends."

"I'm assuming that will make it easier for her to settle in here," Amanda said.

"It should," Mariah confirmed.

"Will she… Hey!" Something bumped Amanda from behind and she lurched forward before regaining her balance. She looked over her shoulder. The black Andalusian stallion stood directly behind her in the corral, his gaze fixed on her, ears pricked expectantly. She could swear his eyes gleamed with mischief.

"Jiggs, behave yourself," Mariah scolded. "He's just playing, Amanda. He does that to us all the time."

"Oh, I see." Amanda smiled weakly. Her perch on the corral meant she was higher than him, but the horse still seemed huge. And when he gently nudged her again, then lipped at the back of her cotton blouse, revealing strong teeth, she jumped back.

"Knock it off, Jiggs," Eli commanded, his voice calm.

Hard hands closed around her waist and swung her down from the corral. She clutched his shoulders, startled, as he lowered her to the ground.

"Thanks," she said shakily, slightly disoriented from the speed with which he'd lifted her and set her down on her feet. The toes of her tennis shoes bumped his boots, and the heated scent of warm male, soap and aftershave hit her in a wave. Belatedly, she realized she was still clutching his shoulders, almost leaning against him, while she stared up into his green eyes. She immediately forced her fingers to let him go and took a step back, his hands sliding from her waist as she moved.

Self-conscious, she glanced around, relieved to find Mariah and Cynthia watching Cade and Zach as they petted Shakira. Amanda was still shaking, but she suspected that had less to do with the horse than with Eli's nearness. He studied her intensely, unnerving her.

"Jiggs really is just playing," he told her. "He wouldn't hurt you."

"Good to know." She managed a smile, trying to regain her composure. In the corral, the big black horse bobbed his head up and down, and she could swear he was agreeing with Eli.

"I have to settle Shakira into her stall before we head down to the studio," Eli said, drawing her attention away from Jiggs. "You can come with me or wait out here, your choice."

"I'll come with you," she told him.

"All right." Heat flickered deep in his eyes before he nodded and stepped away, walking to where his brothers discussed the new mare.

Amanda drew a deep breath. Mariah and Cynthia climbed down from their perch on the corral fence and joined her. Much to Amanda's relief, they didn't appear to have noticed that moment of sexual tension that had flared, hot and alive, between her and Eli.

"I have to get back to the Lodge, Zach," Cynthia called. "I have an appointment with the plumber in twenty minutes."

"I'll drive down with you," Zach told her. "I want to talk to him about adding another bathroom off the lobby area." He clapped Eli on the shoulder. "You've got a beautiful horse here, Eli. Congratulations. Can't wait to see her foals."

"Thanks." Eli's grin flashed white against his tanned face.

"I'd better head out, too," Cade said. "I have to see the accountant about taxes." He handed Shakira's lead to Eli. "We have to talk about how soon we can breed her to Jiggs."

"We'll do that," Eli agreed with a swift smile.

Mariah joined Cade, calling goodbye as they followed Zach and Cynthia toward the trucks parked outside the house across the ranch yard.

"This won't take too long, Amanda." Eli started toward the open barn door, leading Shakira, and Amanda followed.

The interior of the big barn was blessedly shady, much cooler than outside, and redolent with the scents of hay, leather and horses. Eli led the pretty mare down the wide center aisle and into a roomy box stall where loose straw bedding covered the floor, several inches deep.

The gate to the box stall was made with narrow planks, spaced wide enough apart for Amanda to have an excellent view inside.

Eli unsnapped the lead from the mare's halter and turned her loose. She bumped his shoulder with her muzzle and shifted away to explore the stall, reaching the gate to whuff at Amanda. The puff of warm, horse-scented air brushed her face and she lurched back, away from the gate. The mare looked at her with interest and, after waiting a moment, moved on to inspect the rest of the stall.

"She's looking for treats," Eli explained as he unlatched the gate and stepped out beside Amanda. "And she's hoping you've got some."

"What kind of treats?" Amanda trailed after him as he walked to the tack room just inside the main door. The rough walls of the room were hung with coiled lariats, leather reins and other gear she couldn't quite identify. Saddles with their blankets tossed over the seats rested atop sawhorses standing on the concrete floor. Several heavy rubber containers were lined up against one wall. Eli twisted the top off one of them and scooped out grain.

"Why do you keep grain in trash cans?" she asked, curious.

He poured the pale gold grain into a bucket and looked up at her. "Because too many critters, like mice or raccoons, can get into a feed sack. They can't chew through this heavy rubber." He rapped his knuckles on the container nearest him, then dropped the scoop back inside and replaced the lid.

"Oh. Of course."

He glanced sideways at her, a half smile curving his mouth. "I'm guessing you've never spent a lot of time on a ranch or around horses, have you?"

She shook her head, her answer wry. "No—and make that never. I grew up in New York City."

"You didn't have friends or relatives who lived in the country?" he asked, his eyes curious.

"No, I'm afraid not." She studied him as he took an apple from another covered rubber container and lifted a curry brush from a shelf. "Does she like apples?"

"I've never fed her one but most horses do."

She stepped back into the wide aisle, and he followed, closing the door behind them. Together, they walked back down the aisle between the stalls.

"Come on in," Eli told her when they reached Shakira's stall and he opened the gate. "She won't mind."

"Are you sure?" Amanda eyed him dubiously.

"Positive." He stepped inside first and held the gate open.

Unwilling to admit getting this close to the large animal in an enclosed area made her very nervous, Amanda followed him in.

"Just don't come up on her hindquarters without warning," Eli told her, gently shouldering the mare aside to walk to the feeder and upend the grain bucket.

"Why? What will she do?"

"If you startle her, she might kick you."

Amanda immediately stepped back, bumping up against the stall's side wall. Eli looked up and scanned her expression, and a grin lit his face.

"She's never kicked anyone, that I know of," he reassured her. "But generally speaking, you shouldn't walk up behind a horse, a mule or even a cow without letting them know you're there. If you startle them, they're liable to lash out."

"Good to know," Amanda said. "I think I'll just stay over here, away from her hooves."

The mare's head was bent as she ate grain, ignoring both Amanda and Eli.

Eli trailed his hand down the horse's back and over her haunches as he walked around her to reach Amanda.

"Tell you what," he told her. "I'll let you feed the apple to her. You'll instantly become her best friend."

"I'm not sure I want to get that close to her teeth," Amanda said with honesty, eyeing the mare. The sound of equine molars grinding grain was clearly audible.

"She won't bite you," Eli assured her. "Some horses

like to nip a human every now and then, but not Shakira. She has perfect manners." He took a folding knife from his pocket and opened the blade, his movements deft and economical as he cut the apple into slices.

The mare finished the grain, snorting as she checked the feeder for any stray bits, then looked over her shoulder before swinging around to join them. She nuzzled Eli's bicep and bumped his hand.

"Hey, stop that," he told her. "I just told Amanda you're well-mannered. Don't make a liar out of me."

Shakira nickered, her ears pricked forward, her liquid brown eyes fastened with interest on the apple.

Eli laid a slice on the flat of his hand and held it under the mare's muzzle. She immediately lipped it carefully from his palm, strong teeth crunching as she chewed.

"Here, now you try." He held a piece out to Amanda.

"I don't think so." She shook her head, pressing her shoulder blades against the stall wall behind her. "She's got very big teeth."

Eli chuckled, his eyes twinkling with amusement. "Yes, she does. But she won't bite you. Just remember to hold your hand flat and let her take it from you."

She was still not quite convinced. Nevertheless, Amanda stepped forward to hold out her hand and Eli laid a slice of apple on her palm.

"Now, hold it out for her."

Amanda stretched her arm out, uncomfortable with getting any closer to the mare, who suddenly seemed to loom much larger.

Shakira's muzzle brushed her hand and Amanda jerked, surprised at the nibbling movements of the horse's lips.

"No, don't pull away." Eli stepped behind her, his

arms enfolding her to cup one large hand beneath hers, the other gently straightening her fingertips. "And don't curl your fingers, unless you want her to nip one of them," he added.

She turned her head to look back and up at him with disbelief, and he shrugged. She could swear he was trying not to laugh. She shook her head at him and faced the mare.

Even though she wanted to concentrate on Shakira, she couldn't pull her focus away from Eli. She felt surrounded by him. His powerful body was a solid, warm wall at her back. The strength of his arms wrapped around her, and the flex and shift of powerful muscles against her shoulders and down her back, heightened her sexual awareness at the same time he made her feel protected and safe. His palm supported hers, his thumb exerting faint pressure across the ends of her fingertips to keep her fingers from curling. When Shakira lowered her muzzle to lip at the apple slice, Amanda didn't jerk away from the unfamiliar tickle of the horse's lips softly nipping at the sensitive skin of her palm while her teeth delicately closed over the apple.

"She's so soft," Amanda said quietly, astonished at the velvety texture of the mare's muzzle against her hand. Emboldened by the mare's careful claiming of the apple, Amanda stroked her hand down the curve of her nose.

Eli's shoulder pressed Amanda's as he reached out to smooth the mare's forelock to one side, revealing a white star on her forehead. "Pretty, isn't she?" His deep voice rumbled with pride.

The bass tones resonated, shivering through Amanda's midriff and faintly vibrating until her fingertips tingled. She was so physically attuned to him that her skin felt electrified.

"Yes," she replied, her voice soft. "She is."

Immune to their praise, the mare finished chewing the apple and looked for more, dropping her head to nuzzle Eli's hand.

"Greedy." He laughed, dropping another chunk of apple into Amanda's palm. His arms lowered, but he didn't step away from Amanda, their bodies still brushing.

Careful to keep her hand flat, she held out the apple slice to Shakira.

"I can't believe how gentle she is," Amanda said. "It's almost as if she knows she could hurt me."

"She's always had beautiful manners whenever I've been around her," Eli told her. "And I saw her nearly every day for a year."

"I can see why Mariah—and everyone else—was so excited about her arriving," Amanda commented. "She really is special, isn't she?"

"I think so. But then, I'm prejudiced." The quiet, affectionate expression on his face told her volumes about how much he cared for the horse.

"I've never had a pet bigger than a cat," she mused, eyeing the mare's powerful neck, back and haunches. "A pet this big must be quite a responsibility."

"No more than any other animal," he told her, shifting so he could reach the mare. "They all have to be fed, watered and cared for. A cat can just as easily get sick, run up vet bills or get hit by a car if it leaves a safe zone and runs into traffic."

Amanda chuckled. "Somehow I can't see Shakira

running out of my apartment and into New York traffic."

"Well, no." He smiled easily. "But a cat could—and Shakira could get out through a downed pasture fence and wander onto the highway. Granted, her being hurt isn't as likely as if she ran out of an apartment in New York, but still…" He shrugged. "It's all relative."

"I suppose so." Amanda let Shakira lift the last slice of apple from her palm and stroked a hand down her forelock while the mare easily crunched the treat. The black hair was wiry. "Her mane isn't as soft as her muzzle," she commented, testing the springy, rough hair with her fingertips.

"Nor as sleek as her coat," Eli told her, running his hand under Shakira's mane and down the strong muscles of her neck.

They spent another ten minutes or so petting the pretty mare before leaving the barn. Amanda was reluctant to go, savoring Eli's closeness as much as her time with the horse. More so, if she was honest.

As they left the shady interior of the barn for the hot sunshine, a black pickup drove into the ranch yard and parked next to the corral. Amanda noticed the Double Bar T logo emblazoned on the side before the driver's door opened and a man stepped out. He was tall, broad-shouldered, and wore the usual rancher's garb of faded jeans, white T-shirt and dusty cowboy boots. The brim of a straw cowboy hat shaded his face, and mirrored sunglasses hid his eyes.

Beside her, Amanda saw Eli go still with surprise for a second before a smile lit his face.

"It's about time you showed up, Mason," Eli said as

he strode forward, closing the few yards that separated the two men. "Where the hell have you been?"

"I'm not the one who's been gone for years." The stranger grinned and the two shook hands, sharing a tight, one-armed guy-hug before they stepped back. "I was in Nebraska, checking out some Hereford bulls Jed's thinking about buying. Where the hell have you been for the last thirteen years?"

"Pretty much all over the States, and just before I came back, I was in Spain," Eli said.

"That's a lot of traveling." Mason's head turned toward Amanda, his smile friendly. "Did you bring the lady back from Spain with you?" he asked Eli, nodding at her.

Eli's expression was unreadable as he looked over his shoulder and beckoned her closer. "This is Amanda Blake," he said. "She's a writer from New York, working on a book about Mom. Amanda, this is Mason Turner. We went to school together."

"It's nice to meet you, Mason." She glanced sideways at Eli. She'd just watched him greet Mason as if they were longtime good friends, yet he'd subtly tensed when she'd joined them.

"Nice to meet you, Amanda." Mason smiled easily down at her. "So you're a writer. Must be an interesting job."

"Yes," she agreed. "I think so."

"I remember Eli's mother well," he told her. "I'd be glad to tell you about her."

"Yeah, right," Eli said dryly. "You probably remember Mom feeding you cookies and slapping bandages on you when you fell off one of her horses."

"Sure I do," Mason said. "Amanda needs to know

stuff like that if she's going to write a book about your mother. She was much more than an artist who was famous for her sculptures. She was a hell of a woman, too."

"Now, that part you've got right," Eli agreed, a small shadow crossing his face briefly.

"Is Eli helping you with your book?" Mason asked, clearly curious.

"Yes," she said calmly. "He is."

"When he's done, call me and I'll tell you all the stuff he didn't include," he told her, aiming a grin at Eli. "Like how we became legendary for winning brawls at rodeos when we were teenagers."

Amanda could swear the space between her and Eli vibrated with tension. She didn't look at him, certain he'd be frowning blackly at her. He certainly didn't want his friend telling her stories about his life as a teenager, years after his mother died, she thought. That slice of his life was strictly out-of-bounds.

"I doubt I'll have time before I have to go back to New York, but if my schedule frees up, I'll call you, Mason," she said with diplomatic politeness, easing her rejection with a warm smile.

"Anytime." Mason looked at Eli. "Do you have a couple of hours free? I brought a stud colt home from Nebraska and I'd like you to take a look at him."

"I'd like to, Mason, but I promised Amanda we'd spend a couple of hours in Mom's studio." He glanced at his wristwatch. "And I've already used up more than half that time."

"You two haven't seen each other for more than a dozen years," Amanda put in, easily reading the conflicted emotions on Eli's face. "And I have lots of notes to keep me busy today. Why don't we postpone the studio until Saturday morning."

"Are you sure?" Eli studied her, intent.

"I'm positive." She slipped car keys from her pocket and jingled them. "I really do need to work on my laptop today if I'm ever going to catch up."

"All right."

"It was nice to meet you, Mason," Amanda said with a bright smile. "Bye, Eli."

The interior of the rental car was overly warm, despite her having left the windows rolled down. Amanda slid onto the sun-heated seat and started the engine. When she drove away, Eli and Mason were still standing outside the barn, watching her leave.

Mason's gaze left the plume of dust, kicked up by the car as it moved swiftly down the gravel road toward the highway, and fastened on Eli. "Pretty woman," he commented. "I picked up a vibe between you two. Are you dating?"

"No, we're not dating," Eli said shortly, still watching Amanda drive away. "And there's no 'vibe.'"

"Then you wouldn't mind if I asked her out?" Mason asked.

"Yeah, I'd mind." Eli shot him a hard look, which eased as Mason laughed out loud.

"That's what I thought." Mason raised his hands palms out, in a universal "hands-off" gesture. "No problem, Eli. You know I never poach. Not my style."

"Good to know," Eli told him, lifting his hat and settling it lower over his brow. "Are we going to take a look at your colt, or what?"

"Sure." Mason turned with alacrity and the two men walked to his truck. "I'm assuming I'm invited to the barbecue Jed told me the Lodge is having Saturday night?"

Eli sighed deeply. "Yeah, I guess," he growled reluctantly. "It's at the Lodge, starts around six o'clock. And stay away from Amanda." His own adamance surprised him.

Mason burst out laughing. He was still chuckling when they climbed into the truck and drove away.

Chapter Eight

As she drove back to Indian Springs, Amanda couldn't stop thinking about Eli and his friend Mason. The warmth in their greeting spoke volumes about their friendship, which apparently had begun when they were young boys. Yet their conversation seemed to indicate Eli hadn't kept in touch after he left the Triple C.

She frowned, pondering the possible reasons a man would leave his home and never return, nor contact his friends afterward. Personally, she couldn't conceive of any circumstance that would keep her from staying in touch with her family and friends, no matter where her career might take her.

She realized that many men were not great communicators. But to never pick up a phone and call? Not even send an occasional postcard?

And Mason's and Eli's comments made it sound as

if that was what had happened, she thought. They'd had no contact at all.

Curiouser and curiouser. Especially when her observations of Eli had convinced her that he loved the Triple C and everything his presence there entailed—the interaction with his brothers, his obvious love for horses and the land, his affectionate acceptance of Mariah, Cynthia and even Harley and Jane as part of his family.

The whole thing was a puzzle—and Amanda had always been intrigued by puzzles. In fact, she'd never been able to resist the challenge of solving the twists and turns of a good mystery.

And Eli Coulter was a very intriguing mystery.

Eli spent four hours at the studio on Saturday, painstakingly cleaning, polishing and rewelding a small loose piece on a wall sculpture of a mustang mare and her long-legged colt. But Amanda wasn't in the studio with him. She'd called around 9:00 a.m. and told him she wouldn't be able to join him because sixty-year-old Ruby Johnson, a retired English teacher and a close friend of Eli's mother, had agreed to an interview.

Apparently, Ruby had been hard to pin down and Amanda didn't want to give her the opportunity to change her mind.

Since Eli remembered Ruby Johnson very well from high school English classes, he was a little surprised she'd consented to be interviewed at all. The woman was fiercely independent and outspoken, with little patience for interruptions she deemed frivolous.

Ruby must have decided Amanda's request wasn't frivolous, he thought with a grin.

Before ending the call, Amanda had said she'd see him at the barbecue that evening.

Despite the reminder that he'd see her later, Eli found himself missing her presence. The studio felt too quiet—even though Amanda wasn't usually chatty or noisy while she worked. He realized he'd become accustomed to her presence, the subtle scent of her perfume, her murmured thanks when he handed her coffee or the brush of her fingers against his if she was the one offering him a mug.

He wasn't sure he was comfortable missing her.

He wasn't sure how he'd become so accustomed to having her near in the short time they'd been working at the studio.

He frowned at the lighter shade of copper highlighting the mane of the colt, not really seeing the sculpture.

Not touching her was getting harder by the day. He could have shown her how to keep Shakira from nipping her fingers without holding her. But the urge to put his arms around her had been too strong and he'd given in to the need. The press of her body on his when her back rested lightly against his chest, the crown of her head just below his chin—all had combined to test his will to the limit. He'd had to step away from her to keep from turning her in his arms and claiming her mouth.

As it was, he could still feel her soft curves imprinted against him from his chin to his thighs. He hadn't been able to stop himself from lowering his head until he felt her hair, soft as perfumed silk, against his lips, chin and nose. Now he couldn't get the feel and scent of her hair out of his mind, off his skin.

He'd wanted women before, but never like this.

Maybe I should seduce her and get over it, he thought grimly.

Unless that would only make you want her more, a small, dissenting voice murmured in his head.

Not possible, he thought, rejecting the concept that she could become permanently important in his life.

He had to admit she hadn't given him any cause to distrust her, which meant he owed her an apology. Especially after the way she'd politely, but firmly, declined Mason's teasing offer to share secrets of their high school escapades.

Not that Mason would tell her anything he shouldn't. Eli knew him too well for that, and even though they'd gone years without seeing each other, the short hours they'd spent together yesterday had convinced Eli his friend hadn't changed. He was still the same straight-arrow, stand-up guy he'd always been.

But Amanda hadn't known Mason was teasing. If she'd wanted to dig up dirt about the Coulter family, Mason's comments would have dangled bait she couldn't have refused.

No way around it. He had to apologize for doubting her. He'd do it tonight, he thought, maybe after he'd plied her with wine at the barbecue.

In an effort to get his mind off Amanda, he turned on the radio, filling the quiet room with classic rock, and determinedly forced thoughts of hazel eyes and silky brown hair out of his brain.

While Eli was alone in the studio, Amanda was drinking Earl Grey tea and sharing an early lunch with Ruby Johnson.

The energetic retired teacher had salt-and-pepper

hair, sharp brown eyes behind wire-framed glasses, and a toned, petite body.

They ate lunch on the wide porch of Ruby's Victorian home in Indian Springs. The old house had white-painted gingerbread trim decorating its pale yellow exterior. A white picket fence enclosed a jewel-green lawn and flower beds that exploded with brilliant color.

Ruby had been working in her garden when Amanda arrived, and even now, her wide-brimmed hat, gloves and clippers lay on a chair at the far end of the porch, awaiting Ruby's return.

"What made you pick Melanie to write about?" Ruby asked, eyeing Amanda over the rim of a delicate white china teacup.

"I've always loved her work," Amanda replied, stirring sugar into her tea. "And when I wanted to write an article about her for my magazine, I found very little information. I've always planned to write book-length fiction, but I was so intrigued by Melanie's work, I decided to write a biography. I asked my boss for a leave of absence and started researching." She lifted her cup at the surrounding neighborhood. "And here I am."

"Yes, so you are," Ruby said. "And how do you like our little town? It must be very different from New York."

"Very different," Amanda agreed. "But that's part of its charm. I've grown rather attached to Indian Springs in the short weeks I've been here, probably precisely because it *is* so very different from the city."

"That's how Melanie felt," Ruby said pensively. "She loved her life on the Triple C, but every now and then, she equally loved flying off to New York for a gallery opening." Her eyes twinkled and she winked at

Amanda. "I always told her I suspected that was because it gave her an excuse to go shopping and get
dressed up in an evening gown."

"Did her family go with her?" Amanda asked, wondering if Eli had liked visiting the city as a little boy.

"Most of the time." Ruby nodded. "They'd leave one
of their neighbors in charge of the ranch, usually their
friend Wayne Smalley, and take off for New York. I'll
never forget the year they all flew back to attend a cer-
emony when Melanie was given a big award. The boys
all had tuxedos, just like their dad." She smiled fondly.
"I have a picture somewhere that Melanie gave me of all
of them at a party afterward, her holding a gold statue,
the boys and Joseph all beaming ear to ear." Her smile
faded. "Of course, that all changed after she died and
Joseph started drinking."

Amanda went still, fingers freezing with the teacup
almost at her lips. "I didn't realize he had a drinking
problem," she said carefully.

"Huh." Ruby snorted, fixing her with a sharp gaze.
"I suppose the folks you talked to in town didn't tell
you about what happened after Melanie died."

Amanda thought a moment. "I heard details about
the accident that caused her death, but now that you
mention it, no one really had much to say about the
years after she died," she said. She knew there had to
be more to the story but she was well aware of the deal
she'd made with Eli and his family.

"Hard to tell if they would have been truthful if you'd
asked," Ruby commented. "Folks in Indian Springs are
protective about the boys. They didn't have much good
to say about Joseph until the last few years of his life.
And not much then, truth be told."

"I assume Melanie's husband was grief stricken when she died," Amanda prompted. She had an uneasy feeling she knew where this was going, and was unsure whether she should ask, but curiosity and a need to know more about Eli's past were undeniable. She tamped down a guilty feeling.

"I'm sure he was," Ruby agreed with a sharp nod. "But that's no excuse for how he treated his sons. He blamed them for her death. Oh, not that they caused it," she said with a dismissive wave when Amanda audibly caught her breath. "They were playing in the creek. She swung out on a rope tied to a tree branch to join them and the rope broke. She fell and hit her head and died instantly. Joseph turned into a mean drunk after she died—and he was cruel to his sons. If Melanie knew what he did…" She paused, shaking her head. "Well, let's just say she wouldn't be happy."

"What did he do?" Amanda was almost afraid to ask.

"That's for the boys to tell," Ruby said, setting her cup down on its saucer with a snap. "But I can tell you this. Not a one of us who knew them blamed them for leaving when they did. I thought it was honorable of the older ones to stay and band together until Eli was through high school and could leave with them. Says a lot about the brothers that they wouldn't leave him behind to deal with Joseph on his own." She picked up a china plate and held it out. "We've been talking and not eating. Try one of these sandwiches. The filling is vegetarian and fresh from my garden."

"They look delicious." Amanda recognized the clear signal that Ruby wouldn't say more about Joseph and his sons. Still, her words painted a stark picture of a life devoid of parental love and affection in the motherless

Coulter household. It sounded as if the brothers had closed ranks to endure and survive. She felt a wave of thankfulness that Eli's brothers hadn't abandoned him. It spoke volumes about their strength, integrity and loyalty that they'd stayed to support each other until the youngest was able to leave the ranch.

She took one of the small tea sandwiches. "It's wonderful!" she exclaimed, the fresh, rich flavors bursting on her tongue.

Ruby smiled with pride. "It's an old family recipe."

Amanda spent another hour with Ruby, and the older woman shared further anecdotes about Melanie and their mutual support of the library, a local women's book club, the art fair at the school and Melanie's participation in the Parent-Teacher Association. But Amanda didn't ask questions about Joseph Coulter and Ruby didn't offer any more information.

By the time Amanda said goodbye and returned to the hotel, she had dozens of questions bouncing around in her head. She didn't need answers for her book research. But instinct told her that those answers would help unravel the mystery that was Eli.

She had plenty of time to jot down notes about her interview with Ruby before it was time to shower, change and drive out to the Lodge for the barbecue at six. Since she was going directly to the Lodge and not to the Triple C outbuildings, she followed a different road off the highway. Like the ranch road, it was gravel, but it was clearly newer and approached the Lodge from the far side.

Amanda reached the parking lot and left her car, the slanting late-afternoon sun warm on her bare throat, arms and legs. She'd donned a white sundress with little cap sleeves, a square neckline that hinted at the valley between her breasts, a full skirt and nipped-in waist. Bright red sandals matched her wide resin bracelet and hoop earrings. With a red cotton sweater to throw on later, when the sun disappeared and the evening cooled, she felt comfortable yet festive. This was the second time she'd been to the Lodge for a party, she reflected, but how different the circumstances were. This time, she had been invited by the Coulters and didn't feel guilty for crashing the event.

Guests strolled over the lawns and sat in groups on the wicker furniture arranged along the Lodge's wrap-around porch. Amanda followed the walkway that led from the parking lot across the lawn toward the porch.

"Amanda!"

She found Mariah standing with Jane at a huge barbecue grill set up at the bottom of the lawn, beneath the shade of a tree.

She waved and started toward them. She was waylaid halfway there by Mason Turner and three other men.

"Hey, Amanda," he said, flicking a finger at the red sweater she carried over one arm. "I hoped you'd be here tonight."

"Hello, Mason." Amanda swept a quick glance over the other three tall, handsome men. "Don't tell me. Let me guess. These are your brothers, right?"

"How did you know?" The tallest one, by not more than an inch, grinned admiringly at her. "I'm Jed." He jerked a thumb at the other two. "These are my little brothers, Ash and Dallas."

"Little?" Amanda felt her eyes widen. They all stood well over six feet.

"He means younger than him," the one Jed had called

Dallas assured her. He eased forward. "How come I haven't met you before, Amanda? I thought I knew all the pretty women in Indian Springs."

Mason groaned aloud. "Back off, Dallas. She belongs to Eli."

He means it, she thought with amazement. Before she could gather her wits and reply, Dallas gave her a disappointed look.

"I'm sorry to hear that, Amanda. If you change your mind, just give me a call, okay?"

"She's not going to call you, Dallas."

A strong arm slipped around Amanda's waist. She didn't have to hear his amused, easy drawl to know it was Eli. Only Eli caused her body to have that instant, sensitized reaction. She thought back to what Mason had said. Had Eli said anything to him about her?

"She's too smart to be sucked in by a line," Eli continued. He looked down at her, his eyes amused.

"Damn." Dallas looked chagrined. "I was hoping she was pretty *and* stupid."

"The politically correct term is intellectually challenged, Mr. Turner," Amanda shot back with a smile.

The men laughed, including Dallas.

"I told you she was too smart for you, Dallas," Eli said.

"Are there any more at home like you?" Dallas asked, eyeing her with interest.

"I have a sister back in New York but she's married," Amanda told him.

"Unhappily?" he asked hopefully.

"No, she's very happily married."

"Well, darn," he said with a gusty sigh.

"Have you guys eaten yet?" Eli asked, changing the subject when the laughter died down.

"No. We just got here a few minutes ago," Mason replied. "But we could smell barbecue for the last mile. If it tastes half as good as it smells, I can't wait."

"Jane's in charge of the food, so I can guarantee it's good," Eli told him.

They strolled in a group across the lawn. Eli walked by Amanda's side, though his hand had dropped from her waist. She continued to wonder whether he was merely being protective of her or whether Mason's comment was true.

Three hours later, after eating Jane's mouthwatering food, meeting more of Eli's friends and being held in his arms on the dance floor, Amanda was nearly convinced there was more behind Eli's actions than protectiveness.

The sun had long since set behind the buttes in the west, and the lawn and walkways to the Lodge and creek were shadowed. Colorful Japanese lanterns swung from lines suspended from corner poles to crisscross over the dance floor, spilling muted gold light over the few couples there. Beneath the trees edging the lawn, the shadows fell deeper, darker.

Swaying to a slow ballad in Eli's arms, Amanda shivered slightly. Though her faint shudder was in response to the fit of their bodies shifting against each other, he must have thought she was chilled, because one of his arms tightened around her waist, anchoring her against him. His other hand smoothed over the sensitive shape of her back until his fingers cupped her nape.

Tucked against the warmth of his hard body, she felt surrounded by him. Her head lay against his shoulder, her lips nearly brushing the strong column of his throat. Each breath she drew in filled her senses with the faint spicy cologne he wore and a unique scent that seemed to be his alone. She couldn't define it but there was something absolutely seductive and irresistible about the elusive faint aroma: it made her want to bury her face against his throat, stroke her tongue over his pulse to taste him, and drown herself in whatever it was about him that lured her closer.

Despite feeling nearly drugged with the overwhelming masculinity of the man who held her, she realized the deeply sensual impact Eli had on her could prove dangerous. Where could this lead? she wondered hazily. They had an unusual relationship, one that didn't yet include friendship, let alone trust. He'd made it clear he was reserving judgment on her, and if she was honest, she wasn't clear whether she trusted him, either.

She'd never been a woman to indulge a purely physical attraction without the involvement of other emotions, and after learning so much about him, she knew she cared more than she wanted to admit. But she was very much afraid that all Eli felt for her was physical attraction.

With reluctance, she tilted her head back and looked up at him. "I should be getting back to town," she murmured. "I promised Ruby I'd be at her house at 9:00 a.m. tomorrow to go through photos she took of your mother when they worked together on committees at the school."

Eli's arms tightened briefly in protest before they loosened, and he stopped moving to the music. "I wish you didn't have to leave," he said reluctantly, "but I understand."

It wasn't until he stepped back, sliding his hand down her arm to thread his fingers through hers, that Amanda realized they were one of only a few couples on the dance floor. They left the low wooden platform and strolled down the walkway to the parking lot.

"Before you go, there's something I have to say."

Amanda looked sideways at him. The faint glow of the lanterns behind them backlit his profile, casting his face in shadow. "What is it?"

"Do you remember when you said you expected me to apologize for misreading you after I got to know you?" he asked.

"I remember."

"Well, you were right," he said. "I owe you an apology. I'm sorry I didn't trust you to keep to the terms of our agreement."

Amanda laughed, his apology as heartwarming as it was unexpected. "I can't tell you how delighted—and surprised—I am that you're actually willing to admit you were wrong."

"I was wrong about you and for that I apologize," he told her, his deep voice amused. "But I'm still a believer in the basic concept. I wouldn't trust someone unfamiliar until I had sufficient time to get to know them."

Amanda heaved a long, loud sigh. "You're such a cynic, Eli."

They reached her car and she leaned back against the driver's door. "But I do appreciate a man who can admit when he's wrong," she added. She rose on her toes and boldly pressed a quick kiss on his lean cheek. "Thank you."

"You're welcome." He braced his forearms on the car beside her and leaned closer, bracketing her with his body. "I like the way you say thank you." He lowered his head, brushing his mouth against hers.

Amanda caught her breath at the swift flash of electric heat.

"Do you?" she murmured, unconsciously sliding her tongue over her lower lip to capture the warm taste of his mouth.

"Mmm-hmm." His body settled over hers and his lips brushed the curve of her cheek, the arch of her cheekbone, the corner of her mouth before returning to fit carefully, slowly over hers.

He wrapped his arms around her waist, lifting her onto her toes until the curve of her hips cradled the hard thrust of his. Her breasts pressed against the solid wall of his chest, her arms linked around his neck and she felt surrounded by him as their bodies touched, clung, heated against each other from lips to thigh.

Amanda felt as if she'd waited a lifetime for this and she shifted, trying to get nearer although his hard angles were already tight against her softer curves. He groaned, a deep, inarticulate sound of need and arousal, his fingers flexing against her back, gathering her closer. The kiss turned hotter as his tongue stroked hers, sending desire surging through her veins and making her burn.

The world slowed, stopped, narrowed to the press of his mouth against hers. When, at last, he lifted his head, she was breathless and dazed.

"I've wanted to do that since the first time I saw you," he whispered, his voice rough.

"You have?" she said, unable to think coherently, her fingers clenching the warm strength of his bare forearms. "I thought you were only tolerating me because my brother-in-law owns a gallery."

"The gallery has nothing to do with my wanting you."

"Oh." She stared up into his molten green eyes. "I'm glad," she whispered.

"I'm still not crazy about the idea of anyone publicizing my family's life by writing a book," he told her bluntly.

"I can live with that," she replied softly.

He smiled, his teeth a flash of white in the dark night. "Good to know." Then he bent his head and kissed her again, his arms wrapping around her to pull her against him.

Amanda slid her arms around his neck, her fingers threading into the silky soft hair at his nape.

The sound of voices drawing nearer broke them apart. Amanda clung to him, her breath choppy and legs weak, as guests drifted into the parking lot, calling good-night as they broke from groups to reach individual vehicles.

"The party must be over," Amanda said, her voice husky.

"I guess so." Eli stepped back as headlights flashed on, illuminating the parking area. "I'd better let you go."

Don't, she thought, but said nothing.

He pulled open the car door, and Amanda slipped inside, lowering the window as he closed her in.

"I'll see you on Monday," she told him, switching on the engine.

He nodded and stepped back as she reversed out of

her parking spot and joined the line of vehicles leaving the lot. As she drove back to the hotel, she could still feel his lips on hers.

Chapter Nine

Amanda moved through Sunday alternately daydreaming about that incredible kiss and trying to puzzle out why Eli had changed so swiftly. Ultimately, she decided to ask him when she saw him on Monday. Fretting and wondering were driving her crazy and she wasn't a person who could go very long without confronting her problems head-on.

She was determined to have a conversation with Eli the moment she saw him on Monday. But when she drove into the ranch yard a little before 10:00 a.m., his truck wasn't parked in front of the house.

Disappointed, she waited a few moments and then climbed the steps to the front porch and knocked on the ranch house door. But there was no response.

"Where is he?" she muttered aloud, turning to scan the nearby buildings. She couldn't see his pickup truck anywhere. In fact, Zach's and Cade's trucks weren't there, either. The ranch yard seemed deserted, and she wondered if Eli and his brothers were out working cattle or riding fence.

A horse nickered. Jiggs stood at the corral fence, ears pricked as he stared at her.

The big black horse reminded her of Shakira. Perhaps Eli was in the barn with the mare. Amanda left the porch and walked briskly across the gravel ranch yard. The big sliding door stood partially ajar and the barn was blessedly shady and cool when she stepped inside.

"Eli?" she called, waiting for a reply. But the silence in the barn was complete, broken only by the rustle of straw bedding.

Shakira's head appeared over the top of her stall door. She nickered, bobbing her head, and Amanda could swear the horse was glad to see her and asking for company.

She turned back and peered out the open door at the buildings and gravel space once more. There was no sign of Eli. Nothing moved; it was quiet as a tomb. Should she be worried?

Glancing at her watch, Amanda left the doorway and walked into the tack room. She found the apples easily enough but it took longer to locate a knife. A worn but sharp-bladed butcher knife lay on a shelf above the rubber container that held the grain and it sliced the apple with smooth efficiency. Amanda returned it to the shelf, gathered up the apple slices and left the tack room. She detoured to check outside once more, but the wide gravel yard between house and barn was still empty of vehicles and no one was in sight.

As she walked down the aisle, Shakira nickered and shifted, rattling the stall gate.

"Hi, pretty girl," Amanda crooned, laughing when the mare stretched her neck over the gate until she could nudge her muzzle against Amanda's shoulder. "I brought you treats."

Bearing in mind Eli's instructions about feeding the mare, Amanda held out her hand and the mare delicately lipped the apple from Amanda's palm.

Outside the barn and across the gravel yard, Eli stepped out of the machine shop, where he'd been working on his truck, just in time to see Amanda disappear inside the barn. Before he could call her name, she was gone.

He stepped back inside, collected the cowboy hat he'd found for her, and crossed the lot to the barn. As he stepped inside, he heard Amanda talking to Shakira.

"You are such a sweetheart," she crooned, petting the horse and combing her fingers through the wiry black forelock. "No wonder everyone loves you. You're pretty *and* sweet. What's not to love?"

Eli leaned his shoulder against the wall just inside the door and watched Amanda and the mare, grinning at what was clearly mutual affection. Who would have thought the city girl would get so much enjoyment out of his horse?

Shakira leaned into Amanda's touch as she rubbed behind her ears.

"Oh, you like that, do you?"

The mare bent her head, nuzzling and lipping at Amanda's free hand.

"Oh, ick. Stop that. You're getting horse spit on me."

Eli burst out laughing when Amanda scrubbed her palm down her jeans and frowned at the mare.

His laughter brought Amanda spinning around, her startled expression quickly replaced by guilt. He shoved away from the wall and walked toward her.

"Hi," Amanda said with a touch of nervousness. "I, um, I know you told me anyplace beyond the studio was off-limits. But I couldn't find you when I arrived, so I looked for you in the barn, but you weren't here, either. So…I thought I'd spend a little time with Shakira while I waited."

"Don't worry about it," he told her, joining her and patting the mare as she nuzzled his shoulder. "I don't mind. In fact, I think it's kind of cute that you seem to get along so well with Shakira."

"Oh, well…" Amanda shrugged self-consciously. "I fed her an apple. I suspect she loves anybody who feeds her, especially apples."

"Maybe," Eli conceded. "But it looked like the two of you were getting along really well."

Amanda beamed, clearly delighted. "I think she recognized me when I came in," she confided.

"I'm sure she did," he said gravely. He raised his hand to brush her hair back over her shoulder and realized he was holding the cowboy hat. "I almost forgot." He set the hat on her head, pleased when it fit. "I wore it when I was about twelve, I think." He adjusted the hat, tilting the brim back, and cupped her chin. "But it never looked this good on me."

He bent his head, her lips soft and warm beneath his. She leaned into him and he wrapped his arms around her to pull her flush against him. She melted against him, her hands slipping around his neck to hold him close.

The moment was lost when Shakira nudged Amanda's cheek with her damp muzzle.

"Hey!" Amanda jerked back, glaring at the mare and rubbing her hand down her cheek. "Stop that."

Eli grinned, laughing when Amanda frowned at him. "Sorry, honey. This is the downside of having a horse that likes you. They can get messy."

"I'm beginning to learn that," she said wryly, stroking her hand down the mare's nose. She glanced sideways at him, then back at the mare. "We need to talk, Eli."

"Uh-oh." He studied her expression. When a woman said those words, it didn't bode well for a man. "About what?"

Her hand dropped away from Shakira and she turned to face him, her hazel eyes meeting his directly. "I'm confused about what's going on between us. And I don't like being confused."

"I think it's pretty clear," he told her. "I'm attracted to you, and given the way you're kissing me back, I assume you feel the same. Am I wrong?"

"No, you're not wrong, but..." She took the cowboy hat off and ran a hand through her hair in frustration. "I'm a little disoriented by your switch from suspicious-almost-hostile-guy mode to..." She waved a hand between them.

"Guy who wants to take you to bed?" he asked helpfully.

Color flooded her cheeks. "I wouldn't have put it quite so bluntly, but since you said it, yes." She eyed him. "What made you change your mind? Or is this Dr. Jekyll, Mr. Hyde personality disorder normal for you?"

He laughed out loud, then laughed harder when she glared at him. "I'm sorry for laughing at you, but that's funny. That's one of the things I like about you—you have a wicked sense of humor." He tucked a strand of silky brown hair behind her ear. "It's not hard to understand, Amanda. I've been attracted to you since I almost knocked you down at the Lodge opening, but I couldn't be sure of your motives when I learned you were digging into Mom's history for your book." He shrugged. "But you were right. After I spent time with you, it was obvious to me that you're a woman with principles. Continuing to mistrust you didn't make sense anymore."

"Plus, there was the guarantee of the contract that prohibits my writing about the Coulters after the date of your mother's death," she reminded him.

"There is that," he conceded. "But mostly it's because once I had no reason to doubt your integrity, I no longer had to consider you off-limits."

"And that's why you kissed me."

He couldn't tell from either her tone or her facial expression how she felt about that.

"That's why I kissed you *then*," he stressed. "Let's be clear here. I've had a hard time keeping my hands off you from day one."

She studied him for a long moment before she drew in a deep breath and her whole body relaxed. Eli realized she'd been tense, her hands clenched at her sides.

"All right," she said with a decisive nod. "I can accept that."

"Good." He closed the slight distance between them and reached for her.

"Wait." She held up one hand, palm out, stopping him.

"What?" he asked, impatient to pick up where they'd left off before Shakira interrupted them.

"I've never had a relationship with a man that began with hostility," she told him. "I'd like to shift gears and go back to the getting-to-know-you part, where we aren't enemies, but we aren't kissing friends yet."

"What?" He frowned at her.

"Seriously," she told him. "I'm feeling a little disoriented by all of this and need a little time to adjust, okay?"

He sighed and scrubbed his hand down his face. "All right." But he wasn't happy about it. Now that he knew how it felt to hold her, it was killing him not to touch her.

"Good." She smiled sunnily at him. "On a totally different subject...I was thinking that Shakira needs a more glamorous halter. Something that looks Spanish, with silver conchas, maybe. What do you think?"

"It's not a bad idea." He narrowed his eyes, considering. "In fact, I'm pretty sure we have a couple of halters with conchas that belonged to Mom."

"You do? I don't remember seeing them in the tack room."

"No, you wouldn't have. Most of Mom's stuff is upstairs."

"Upstairs?" She glanced around the barn, zeroing in on the flight of rough plank stairs just to the right of the entry door. "I assumed you stored hay up there."

"We do." Eli patted Shakira's cheek one last time and cupped Amanda's shoulder to turn her with him. "But we also store other stuff up there," he told her as they walked back down the wide aisle lined with stalls until they reached the stairs. "There's a fair-size room up here filled with Mom and Dad's horse gear," he added as they climbed the stairs to the second floor of the barn.

Amanda followed him across the rough planks of the flooring toward the far end of the big space.

"I thought this would be filled with hay," she commented.

"It will be in the fall," he told her. He pointed at the huge double doors that took up most of the wall ahead of them. "Those doors open out and we off-load hay bales straight into the loft."

They stopped in front of a normal-size door. Amanda turned slowly, taking in the expanse of wide bare boards beneath the steep pitch of the roof.

"It must take a lot of hay bales to fill this space. It's huge."

Eli ran his fingers along the top ledge of the door and found a key. He glanced at Amanda. "It holds a lot of hay, but not enough for all the cattle we used to run on the Triple C. We have a second hay shed in back of the barn."

"A ranch is really like running a family-owned manufacturing company, isn't it?" she asked him.

"It definitely involves a lot of the same business practices and concerns," he agreed. "I like most of the work, except for the financial details, like bookkeeping. Luckily, Zach not only enjoys finances, but he's good at them."

"It sounds as if between you and your brothers, you have all the different talents needed to run a successful business—or in this instance, a successful ranching operation."

He nodded. "I'd say so." The lock gave under the

key, rasping as the mechanism slowly moved, as if rusty from lack of use, and Eli pushed the door inward. "Here we are." He flipped the light switch on the wall to the right of the doorjamb and stood back to let Amanda enter the room first.

"Wow." Her voice held astonishment.

Eli hadn't been in the room since he'd returned to the Triple C, and as he scanned the walls and floor, he understood Amanda's stunned exclamation.

Like the tack room downstairs, the rough board walls were lined with rows of leather bridles and headstalls, halters and chaps. There were also riding quirts and longer whips used for driving teams of horses. All of the tack was fancier than the everyday things kept in the room below.

And row upon row of sawhorses lined the floor, holding saddles and blankets.

"Did your parents actually use all of this?" Amanda asked.

Hands propped on his hips, Eli slowly turned in a half circle, scanning the items on the walls and floor. "Yeah." He nodded finally. "They did. When Mom was alive, she and Dad loved doing what they called 'treasure hunting.' If something was old and historic, Mom wanted to buy it and bring it home. They gathered multiple collections, one of which was old West wagons, buggies, stagecoaches, that kind of thing. Mom not only rode, but she loved to hitch up horses to a buckboard or buggy and take us kids on a picnic. So most of this stuff—" he waved a hand that encompassed the contents of the room "—was used by her at one time or another. And apparently, like the rest of her things, Dad kept the collection intact."

"Are all the old buggies and wagons still here on the ranch as well?" Amanda asked with interest.

"As far as I know, they are. Dad put up a building especially to house them. Cade and Zach don't want to unlock it until Brodie gets home so we can all go in together."

"When do you expect Brodie to come home?" she asked, running a testing hand over the smooth wool of a nearby Pendleton blanket.

"That's the million-dollar question. None of us have the answer." He didn't tell her he wasn't sure Brodie was ever coming back to the Triple C. Instead, he started across the floor to reach a group of bridles and halters hanging on the wall. "Mom was partial to this bridle." He slipped the web of connected black leather straps decorated with tarnished silver conchas off its peg. "And this halter." He moved a step to the left to reach a matching halter. He walked back to Amanda with the leather tack. "They don't look so great now, but once we clean the tarnish off the silver and oil the leather, they'll be good as new."

"Excellent." She smiled at him. "I'll help clean them. Are you taking them to the studio?"

He fought the urge to bend his head and cover her mouth with his. Instead, he started toward the open door. "Might as well. Are you ready to leave?"

She nodded and they went back downstairs. Eli followed her out of the barn and into the sunlight. He wasn't sure how the hell he'd been conned into a situation that required him not to touch her again.

"How long is it going to take for you to get adjusted to us being more than friends?"

"I'm not sure." She glanced sideways, her gaze focused on his mouth. "Not too long."

"Thank God," he muttered.

"Where's your truck?" she asked.

"In the machine shop." He pointed at the building, half the size of the barn, to their right. "I'll meet you down at the studio."

"All right." She walked away toward her car.

Eli stood still, staring after her, following the sway of her hips in the snug jeans, the sun glinting off gold streaks in her brown hair beneath the straw cowboy hat.

"Damn." He sighed. He hoped to hell she got used to the truce between them and soon. He doubted he'd make it very long before kissing her again.

Chapter Ten

Over the next few days, Eli tried to exercise patience and give Amanda space. Each day they walked to the Lodge to have lunch and he found himself relaxing, watching how well she fit in with Mariah, Cynthia and Jane. They took Harley to see the puppies several times, and just as Amanda had fallen in love with Shakira, she seemed to be equally enthralled with the eight rottweiler puppies.

At noon on a Tuesday, they walked to the Lodge for lunch as had become their habit.

"Do you think it will rain?" Amanda asked him, tilting her head back to look up at the gray clouds piling up on the horizon.

"Not today," Eli told her. He glanced sideways at her. She seemed remarkably calm while he was growing more short-tempered by the day. He loved spending time with her, but keeping a leash on his desire was growing increasingly difficult. Cold showers weren't doing anything to cool his need for her. Her hair shifted over her shoulder, leaving the curve of her arm and the tender nape of her neck bare. He drew in a deep breath and fought down the urge to bend nearer and touch his lips to the soft skin. Distracted, he struggled to remember what he'd been planning to say. "But maybe tomorrow. I hope it pours for a couple of days. The pastures and fields can use the rain."

They reached the Lodge and entered the kitchen.

"Eli says it could rain tomorrow, Jane," Amanda said. "You might not have to water the garden for a day or two."

"That's good news." Jane moved from stove to counter, carrying steaming bowls. Amanda, Mariah and Cynthia joined her while Eli filled a pitcher with ice-cold water.

The conversation was brief until plates were emptied and they sat with coffee, hunger sated.

Zach walked into the room, wiping grease from his hands with a towel.

"Eli," he said with a grin. "You're just the person I need."

"What's broken?" Eli asked, eyeing the black streaks on his brother's shirt.

"One of the pipes in the upstairs hall bathroom has a leak. Come help me figure out which one."

Eli groaned. "Why is it I'm helping you again? You hauled me out of bed at four this morning to chase cows that were out of the pasture. Couldn't you drag Cade up here to help you with plumbing?"

Even as he spoke, he was standing and carrying his plate and utensils to the sink.

"I won't be long, Amanda," he told her as he joined Zach and the two left the room.

Cynthia's smile was warm as she sipped her coffee. "It's so nice that Eli's here. Zach insisted he wasn't worried, but I know he was relieved when the detective finally located him."

"I didn't realize his brothers didn't know he was working in Spain," Amanda said.

Mariah shook her head. "They normally kept in touch every few months or so, if not in person, at least by phone, but evidently Eli didn't check in when he was out of the country."

She gave Cynthia a sympathetic look. "Cade was worried about not hearing from Eli, too."

"I can't imagine not calling and talking with my sister at least once a week," Amanda commented. "Maybe guys just don't feel the need to stay as closely connected to their siblings."

But if infrequent and sporadic contact equaled staying in touch to Eli and his brothers, what did that say about his ability to connect intimately with anyone? With her?

Worry pinched her heart and she realized that if she were to see or hear from Eli only every now and then, it would devastate her.

Mariah shrugged. "Hard to say. Men can be a real puzzle."

"Now, there's an understatement," Cynthia said dryly.

The back door of the kitchen, which led to the deck, opened suddenly. The man just outside stood motionless, framed in the doorjamb. The sun at his back haloed his body with gold and dazzled Amanda's eyes. All she could make out was the familiar tall, broad shape of a man with coal-black hair.

"Eli?" Surprised, she stared at him, squinting against the bright sunlight. "I thought you and Zach went upstairs."

The man didn't respond. Instead, he stepped across the threshold and into the kitchen, stopping abruptly.

"You're not Eli." Amanda stared, frowning as she assessed the black hair and craggy features, the green eyes. His shoulders were broad, but the Western, pearl-snapped cowboy shirt he wore hung a bit loose on his frame, as if he'd lost weight since he'd bought it. He wore jeans on his long legs, the faded denim worn white at stress points, and black cowboy boots on his feet.

He held a carved wooden cane in one hand.

Recognition swept Amanda.

"You must be Brodie."

He nodded, thick-lashed green eyes narrowing over her. "I'm looking for Eli or Cade." He scanned the kitchen, his gaze flicking over Jane, standing still and silent at the stove, and then Mariah and Cynthia, perched on stools at the counter. His impersonal stare seemed to dismiss them before it returned to Amanda. "Or Zach. Are they here?"

"Zach and Eli are upstairs." Cynthia slipped from her stool. "I'll get them."

"Would you like to sit down?" Amanda ventured as Brodie started across the room, apparently following Cynthia.

"No." The word was brusque.

"But…" Amanda wanted to tell him he should rest, that Cynthia would bring his brothers to him, but the look he gave her stopped the words in her throat. His green eyes were so dark they were nearly black, and they rejected any overtures. He clearly didn't want sympathy. But watching him limp, leaning heavily on the cane, was painful. She wanted to jump up and lend her shoulder for him to lean on.

He was almost to the hallway door when Eli and Zach returned with Cynthia.

"Brodie." Eli grabbed him in a hard male hug, his face wreathed in smiles. "Damn, why didn't you tell us you were coming?"

"Hey, bro." Zach waited until Eli stepped back before wrapping his arms around Brodie in a brief hug. "Yeah, you should have called us. I would have killed a fatted calf."

Zach's allusion to the prodigal son being welcomed home brought a fleeting smile to Brodie's face.

"You've probably already got a couple in the freezer," he said dryly.

"True." Eli pulled out a stool at the counter. "Sit down and tell us about the trip."

Brodie eased his hips onto the tall seat, stretching out his stiff left leg and hooking the cane over the edge of the tiled counter.

"Not much to tell. I left California a week ago. A friend helped me load my truck and he did most of the driving until I dropped him off at his place in Idaho two days ago."

Eli whistled, a soft, low sound. "Your doctors said you could ride over a thousand miles in a truck? The leg must be a lot better."

Brodie's half smile was part grimace. "I wouldn't say that. But," he said with a shrug, "it is what it is. I couldn't stay in a convalescent hospital forever."

"We're glad you're here," Zach told him. "Are you hungry? We just had lunch but I'm sure Jane could whip something up for you."

Brodie shook his head. "No, I just wanted to check in and let you know I'm here. I'm guessing there's room for me to stay at the house?"

"I'm the only one there most nights," Eli told him. "So there's lots of space."

"Good. I'll head on up there." Brodie gathered his cane and stood.

Amanda didn't miss the flash of pain that moved over his features before his face became blank. She flicked a quick worried glance at Eli. In a barely perceptible movement, he shook his head, warning her away.

"Eli and I will go with you," Zach said. "I need to track down Cade and talk to him about some work he wants done on the tractor."

Brodie nodded briefly and headed for the door, his limp more pronounced than when he'd entered. Amanda wondered if sitting had made the leg stiffen more.

"I'll see you tomorrow, Amanda?" Eli asked. She nodded and his eyes warmed before he followed Brodie, holding the door open for him. Zach halted when Cynthia stopped him with a hand on his arm, going up on tiptoe to whisper in his ear. He nodded and pressed a quick kiss on her mouth before following his two brothers.

The four women in the kitchen were silent, listening to footsteps as the men crossed the deck. The rhythm of Eli's and Zach's strides was slower than normal, keeping time with the step and thump of Brodie and his cane.

"Whew," Cynthia said when the sound of a truck engine turning over reached their ears. "So that's Zach's brother, the rodeo star." She shook her head. "He looks a little scary."

Amanda knew exactly what Cynthia meant. Even though he'd clearly lost weight recently, he was still a big man and the pain lines bracketing his mouth only added to the impression of darkness that he exuded. He seemed unapproachable.

"I suggested Zach move a bed downstairs for him," Cynthia continued. "All the bedrooms are upstairs but there's a sunroom off the living room that's close to the downstairs bathroom. I don't see Brodie climbing the stairs to the second floor."

"No, neither do I," Amanda said. "Not right away. I wonder if the leg will get better or if he'll always need the cane."

"I hope not." Cynthia's blue eyes were grave. "Zach tells wonderful stories about Brodie, and nearly all of them involve something physical, like riding horses or bulls. I can't imagine how awful it must be for him to lose that part of his life."

"I know," Amanda said softly. "Eli rarely talks about his childhood without commenting on some exploit of Brodie's." She stared thoughtfully at the door. "I wonder how he'll fit in here, now that he's back."

"I don't know but I'm sure his brothers are glad he's home," Cynthia said with conviction.

Amanda knew from comments Eli had made that all the brothers were worried about Brodie. "Now that he's finally here, I hope he stays."

"I hope so, too," Mariah said, a smile lighting her face. "Just the other night, Cade was telling me about how much fun they used to have over the holidays when they were boys. Their mother held Christmas celebrations at the Lodge and it was clearly unforgettable for all of them. I told him I want to celebrate Christmas here this year, and now that Brodie is back, all the brothers will be home for the holidays."

"That's a wonderful idea, Mariah," Cynthia declared, her eyes bright with enthusiasm. "We can block out guests for a long weekend and have everyone stay in the suites upstairs so we're all together."

"Perfect," Mariah told her.

Amanda didn't comment. It was already August and she'd be back in New York long before December arrived with its celebrations. The realization made her unaccountably sad. She glanced away from Cynthia and Mariah, who radiated happy anticipation, and found Jane. Suddenly realizing the chef had been unusually quiet, Amanda felt guilty. "I'm sorry, Jane. We're underfoot and keeping you from your work, aren't we?"

"No." Jane's smile was brief and her face seemed paler than usual. "Not at all."

"Nevertheless, I should head back to town and get out of your way." Amanda stood, gathered her dirty dishes, and carried them to the sink to rinse and tuck into the dishwasher.

"I'd better get back to work, too," Cynthia said. "See you tomorrow, Amanda. Come into the office and we'll go over those invoices when you have a moment, Jane."

Cynthia had disappeared into the hallway that led to her office and Mariah was still rinsing her dishes when Amanda left the Lodge by the back door. As she walked briskly down the gravel road on her way to the studio, she wondered why Jane had seemed upset by Brodie's appearance. She hadn't commented or made any overt gestures to indicate she was anything other than an observer of a family reunion. But Amanda had picked up on a wary tenseness in Jane that seemed odd, given she'd never met Brodie before.

Maybe Jane was just reacting to the darkness that seemed to hover around Brodie, Amanda thought. As Cynthia had noted, Brodie's appearance was a little scary. Although personally, Amanda thought it was more the remote expression on his face, coupled with the barely leashed anger that she'd seen in his eyes, that made him seem intimidating.

I wonder if he'll answer some questions about his mother, she thought, hope spiking for a moment before she considered and rejected the idea. *Not likely.*

Even if she had the courage to ask him, which wasn't going to happen in this lifetime.

Nothing connected to the Coulter brothers was easy, she reflected later that evening, as she climbed into bed.

She was afraid she was more than just attracted to Eli.

It felt too much like she was falling in love—and she had no idea if he felt the same. She'd felt a connection to him from the first moment they met, and that scared her.

She stared up at the ceiling. It was clear Eli felt something for her, but wanting to take her to bed wasn't the same as having deeper feelings. In some ways, Eli seemed as blocked off as Brodie. Maybe she was kidding herself to think they could have a real relationship.

She desperately hoped she wasn't falling in love alone.

When they left the women at the Lodge, Brodie didn't refuse Eli's offer to drive his brother's truck back to the ranch house. And Eli and Zach ignored Brodie's insistence that he could climb the stairs to a bedroom. Instead, they installed him in the living room, stretched out on the long leather sofa, while they wrestled a bed downstairs and set it up in a room on the first floor. Once employed as a sunny sitting room by their mother, it had long been used for storage and was currently nearly empty. Within an hour, they'd put sheets and blankets on the bed and hauled in the few bags and boxes they found in Brodie's truck.

Brodie was sound asleep on the sofa and they decided to leave him undisturbed, returning to the Lodge to finish fixing the plumbing. Cade joined them before they were done. He had been by the house to see Brodie and agreed with Eli and Zach that their brother didn't look well, even though he was walking.

The following morning Eli woke to the sound of rain pounding on the roof and running off the eaves. After showering and dressing, he went downstairs and filled the coffeemaker with water. The pot had just finished brewing when Brodie entered the kitchen. His hair sleep-tousled and his jawline unshaven, he was dressed in loose sweatpants, a T-shirt and socks.

"Morning." Eli scanned his brother's drawn face and took down mugs. He handed a steaming mug to Brodie without comment and followed him back into the living room, where the big leather recliner allowed Brodie to elevate his leg.

Eli switched on the television to a news station and sat down on the sofa, stretching out his long legs to prop his boots on the scarred coffee table.

When their mugs were empty, Eli went back into the kitchen and brought the thermal carafe into the living room, refilled both their mugs and slouched on the sofa again.

It was a half hour before Brodie spoke. "It's raining."

"Yeah," Eli agreed.

"What are you doing today?"

"Hanging with you for a while," Eli said, flashing him a grin. "Amanda shows up around ten and we'll go work in the studio for three or four hours. Might stay longer today since it's raining and I don't feel like getting soaked."

"No emergency that has to be taken care of outside?" Brodie's voice rasped, amused.

"Nothing that can't wait until the rain stops."

"You never did like getting wet unless you were swimming," Brodie commented idly. "Reminded me of a damn cat."

"Huh," Eli grunted. "What are you up to today?"

"Not much," Brodie said with feeling. "The road trip did a number on my leg. I think I'll hang around the house."

"Good plan."

By the time ten o'clock arrived, Eli had cleared the kitchen and Brodie was asleep, stretched out on the sofa after taking pain pills. He kept straining his ears for the sound of Amanda's car arriving. Not that he was anxious, he told himself. But when he heard the crunch of tires on gravel, he bolted for the door.

Rain ran from the brim of his hat as he stopped at the car to talk to Amanda, who rolled down the window to speak to him.

"Let's take my truck," he told her. "We'll leave your car here. The driveway to the studio can be muddy when it rains and I don't want you getting stuck."

"All right." She gathered her things and they hurried to his truck.

"Wow, this weather is crazy," she said when they were tucked inside the cab, rain dampening her jacket and hair. "Thunder and lightning and downpours."

"Well, it's good for the fields," he told her as he backed the truck and headed away from the house. He glanced sideways at her, taking in her loose hair and light jacket over blue jeans and boots.

She waggled a brown paper bag. "I had the café pack a lunch for us this morning so we wouldn't have to go out if it's still raining at noon."

"I like a woman who plans ahead," he said with approval.

"How's your brother?" she asked. "Is he feeling better this morning?"

"He took pain pills and I left him sleeping on the couch," Eli said, turning off the gravel road and easing the big pickup down the short dirt driveway to the studio. "He looks like hell, but I'm glad he's here and not a thousand miles away in California." He braked, parking close to the front door, and switched off the engine. "Stay put. I'll come around and get you."

Amanda gathered her things and prepared to dash to the studio. But when Eli opened the truck door, he reached in and plucked her off the seat, swinging her out of the truck in his arms before she could protest and shoving the door closed with his shoulder. His long strides quickly reached the studio and he bent his knees to turn the knob. Then they were inside, the door closed behind them to shut out the damp.

Eli set her on her feet, letting her legs slide down the length of his while his arm at her back kept her close.

This hands-off policy was killing him. He hoped it was getting to her, too.

Then he frowned, raising his hand to test her hair between thumb and forefinger.

"You're wet," he said, his deep voice rumbling. He released her and disappeared into the bathroom. "Take off your jacket and anything else that's wet."

She wondered with amusement just how much of her clothing he thought she would shed, but then he was back, a thick towel in hand.

"Turn around," he told her.

She obeyed and felt his hands as he carefully blotted the towel against the damp ends of her hair.

"That'll do," he muttered. "Why aren't you wearing the hat I gave you?"

"It wasn't sunny out," she told him as he took her purse and the paper bag from her hands and set them on the workbench. "I didn't think about wearing it to keep the rain off."

"I suppose you use an umbrella at home." He took her jacket and hung it over the back of a chair, then shrugged out of his own wet coat. He removed his hat and hung it on a hook just inside the door before slinging the coat over the back of a second chair.

They settled to work, he at the workbench, she at her table. This time, for some reason, the silence did not seem companionable. Eli was about ready to jump out of his skin. That brief physical contact with Amanda had put all his nerve endings on high alert.

Finally it was lunchtime. Eli suggested they eat on the sofa. He was clearly a glutton for punishment, he thought.

Amanda had brought roast beef sandwiches, the

café's homemade potato chips, thick-sliced dill pickles and a variety of small pastries.

"I forgot to bring anything to drink," Amanda told him as she took napkins and plastic forks from the bag.

"There might be something in the fridge. I'll check," he told her. "If not, we can always have water or coffee." He reached the kitchenette and peered into the fridge. "We're in luck. I found a bottle of wine." He rummaged in a drawer for an opener, removed the cork and carried the bottle back to the sofa, along with two squat tumblers. "No wineglasses, so we'll have to make do with these."

"I don't mind."

A half hour later the remains of their lunch were strewn on the table and Amanda sat beside Eli on the comfortable sofa, a tumbler half full of wine in one hand. Her feet were curled beneath her, while his long legs were stretched out, stockinged feet propped on the edge of the coffee table. His boots sat at the end of the sofa, next to her much smaller ones. It was a cozy picture—but Eli was feeling anything but serene. What would she do if he reached over and...

"I talked to Lindsey this morning, before I drove out," she said, breaking him out of his reverie. "Tom was at the house and I spoke with him briefly, too. He reminded me that the gallery exhibit and auction are only three weeks away." She looked at Eli. "And my return ticket to New York is in five days."

His face tightened. "Stay until the gallery showing in a few weeks. We'll fly back together."

"I wish I could, but I can't. Mom and Dad's anniversary is in a week and I promised I'd be there for the celebration. Lindsey planned a surprise party with all their friends." She shook her head. "I can't miss it."

"I understand," he said quietly. "I wish you didn't have to leave, but having parents to celebrate with is a big deal."

He leaned forward and set his empty tumbler on the table.

"We still have five days," she said in an attempt to lighten the mood. "I'd be glad to help you to pack your mother's pieces for shipping. And then you'll be in New York in three weeks. You're going to like Tom and you'll love his gallery and..."

Eli laid his finger over her lips, hushing her words.

"We only have five days, Amanda," he said bluntly. His green eyes darkened, intent on hers. "I'd like to spend them doing more than talking."

She caught her breath, uncertain. She was torn between taking that step, saying the words that would free him of restraint and potentially move them closer, or remaining silent and staying safe behind her self-imposed wall.

"Say yes, Amanda," he urged softly. His thumb stroked slowly, seductively, over the plump curve of her lower lip.

She felt him lift the wine tumbler from her hand and set it on the table without taking his gaze from hers. She curled her hands over his biceps, bare beneath his T-shirt, and felt the tension in his powerful body.

She had the sudden conviction that this, their coming together, had been inevitable from the first moment at the Lodge, when she'd turned and looked up into his green, green eyes.

Any remaining doubts fled.

"Yes," she murmured, her body leaning into his, her mouth nearly brushing his lips.

It was like flipping a switch. Eli didn't hesitate. He slid his fingers into her hair, one hand cupping her head while the other caught her waist to tug her nearer as his mouth covered hers.

She slid her hands around his neck, her fingers spearing into the thick silk of his hair at his nape.

His lips seduced hers, and when his tongue stroked her lower lip, coaxing the seam of her mouth to part, he tasted of the wine they'd drunk and a hotter, darker flavor that was instantly addictive.

Her fingers flexed, holding him closer, and he groaned, shifting her until she lay flat on the wide sofa. His weight lowered over her, his powerful thighs against hers, the hard proof of his arousal nestled in the cove of her hips. Now that they'd started, they both seemed powerless to stop.

He tugged the hem of her knit top higher and stroked his hand over the exposed skin of her rib cage, above the waistband of her jeans, before his warm palm closed over the curve of her lace-covered breast.

Amanda groaned aloud and twisted, trying to get closer. Eli tore his mouth from hers and stood, pulling her to her feet in front of him.

"We've both got too many clothes on," he muttered.

As he unbuttoned her jeans and shoved them down her hips, she fumbled with his shirt, managing to push it off his shoulders before he tugged her hands away so he could pull her cotton top off over her head.

The moment her hair tumbled back to brush her shoulders, she reached for him, but he caught her hands, holding her still as he stared at her. His eyes were green fire as his gaze raked her from head to toe, returning to linger on her breasts.

"You're beautiful," he said, his voice harsh, tight with arousal. He released her hands and flicked open the front clasp of her bra, his warm, bare palms cupping her breasts.

She arched into his touch, her flesh so sensitive she caught her breath.

Eli caught her when her knees gave way and she swayed, wrapping her arms around his waist and pressing against him, the warm, hard muscles of his chest cushioning her breasts.

He eased her down onto the sofa and knelt to pull off her socks, jeans and panties. Then he stood and, with swift, jerky movements, took a small square wrapper from his pocket and tore it open. Then he unsnapped his jeans and shoved them down his legs, taking black boxers with them, before he rolled on protection and joined her on the sofa.

Before Amanda had time to absorb the details of his bare, fully aroused, powerfully male body against hers, his arms wrapped around her, his hair-roughened thigh nudging between hers as his mouth once again took hers.

She wanted to explore and test the silky warm skin over the powerful muscles that lay over hers, but there was no time. Passion and lust roared out of control and all she could do was hang on as Eli nudged, pushed, then sank home. She caught her breath, adjusting to the invasion, but then he moved, surging against her, and she lost the ability to think. She could only feel as sensation and pleasure swept her under.

Chapter Eleven

They spent the afternoon curled up on the sofa, listening to the rain on the roof and making love. When the day darkened outside and early dusk fell due to the rain and dark clouds, they reluctantly dressed and prepared to leave.

"Stay over," Eli murmured, his lips moving against her hair. "I'll make you breakfast in the morning."

She leaned back in the circle of his arms to look up at him. "You can cook?"

"I make a great Spanish omelet," he told her. His hands settled low at the back of her waist and he tugged her closer, until her hips and thighs were snugged against his. "Stay."

"Will your brother mind?" Amanda asked, torn between wanting to stay and wondering whether she would be wiser to step back from the whirlwind pace of intimacy with Eli.

"Brodie? No. Why would he?" He glanced at his watch. "It's a little after five. I'll call Jane and have her throw some food together so we can pick it up before going up to the house."

"Won't she be in the middle of the dinner rush? I'm not sure we should do that to her."

"She won't mind. She always has a family version of whatever she's serving at the Lodge. Zach and Cynthia use the service often—probably not as often as I do, since I hit her kitchen nearly every night," he added with a half grin. "Come on," he coaxed. "Stay for dinner at least."

"I'll stay for dinner," she said, giving in. "But I'm not sure about staying the night. All my things are at the hotel."

"I'll loan you a toothbrush," he told her.

"Eli," she protested. "I'm not sure…."

"Let's talk about it after dinner," he said, catching her hand and tugging her after him toward the door. "I'm starving."

They bundled into coats and Eli swung her up in his arms once more, insisting on carrying her across the muddy drive to the truck. The rain beat a tattoo on the roof of the cab as he drove to the Lodge, leaving the engine running while he ran into the kitchen, returning in short moments with two large brown paper bags.

"Jane gave us enough for three, in case Brodie hasn't eaten yet." He handed her the bags and backed out of the parking slot, driving down the service lane at the rear of the Lodge and onto the gravel ranch road that took them back to the ranch house.

Just as Eli parked and switched off the truck engine outside the house, the rain let up.

"You have impeccable timing, Mr. Coulter," Amanda told him, pushing open the passenger door and jumping out.

Eli joined her and they ran up the sidewalk to the porch. A gust of wind caught them as Eli opened the door, pelting them with raindrops as they hurried inside.

"Nice weather for ducks," Eli muttered as he slammed the door.

"But not for humans," Amanda laughed, shaking raindrops from her hair and coat.

"You two look wet," Brodie said from the depths of the recliner in the living room.

"It's pouring out there," Eli told him. "We stopped at the Lodge and Jane sent enough food for all of us. Are you hungry?"

"Always," Brodie answered promptly.

Eli and Amanda opened the bags of food on the coffee table, fetching plates and utensils from the kitchen, and joined Brodie to eat dinner. Afterward, Eli set up a folding table next to the recliner and the three of them played poker, Eli and Brodie complaining loud and long when Amanda had a run of beginner's luck and took most of their coins.

"I like your brother," Amanda told Eli as she climbed into bed later that night. She wore one of his T-shirts in lieu of pajamas and it hit her midthigh, the neck opening nearly slipping off one shoulder.

"You should have met him before the accident," Eli said. "He's always been edgy, but since he came home, he's darker."

She curled her legs under her, turning to face him. "You're worried about him, aren't you?" she said softly.

"We all are. Rodeo's been his life since he was a kid. Without it..." Eli shook his head.

Amanda leaned closer, smoothing her fingertip over the two small frown lines that drew a V between his eyebrows, easing them away. "He'll find his way," she assured him. "All of you seem to love this amazing land and I can only assume Brodie feels the same. That will make all the difference. He has a chance to heal here."

"I hope you're right." He cupped her chin in one big palm. "Come here." He wrapped his arms around her, pulling her down on top of him. "I'm guessing this bed is a lot more comfortable than the sofa at the studio. Let's test it."

She laughed as his lips met hers. And then there was only heat and passion while thunder rolled and lightning flashed outside the window.

The next five days flew by much too fast. Amanda and Eli didn't talk about her leaving; instead, they spent every moment possible in each other's company. And when it was time for her to leave, she refused to let him take her to the airport. She wasn't good at saying goodbye and she didn't want his last image of her to be with tears running down her face, her eyes turning red as she sobbed. Eli reluctantly let her have her way, but only because he knew he'd be joining her in New York for the auction in just over two weeks.

Fortunately for both of them, there were telephone calls. Lots of telephone calls. They talked several times a day, any time of the day, but they always, without fail, called each other before going to sleep. This was reassuring to Amanda. This was the same man who had gone an entire year without talking to his brothers. Clearly, he felt the need to talk to *her*.

A week after Amanda returned to New York, the phone rang just after ten and she put down her book, smiling as she took the phone from the bedside table. She didn't need the quick glance at caller ID to tell her who was calling.

"Hello, Eli," she said.

"Hi, honey. I wish you were here. Or I was there."

"What's wrong?"

"It's too quiet around here," he said, his voice a deep rasp. "Even my horse is moping."

"I'm so sorry, Eli." Delight bubbled and she laughed. "Are you trying to tell me in a very roundabout way that you miss me?"

"I guess I am." He sounded surprised but she heard the thread of amusement in his voice.

"I miss you, too, and I wish I was there. Or that you were here," she added. "Why don't you catch an earlier flight? You could be here tomorrow. We could order in and spend the day catching up."

"Catching up?" He laughed. "I like the sound of that. It's been a week since you left. We have a lot of catching up to do—in bed and out."

"I wish Montana wasn't so far away from New York," she said, frustrated that they were separated by so many miles.

"So do I, honey, so do I." He sighed, a gusty sound of frustration. "Hey, Tom called today. He had a question about hanging one of Mom's wall sculptures. I told him we can talk about it when I get there but I think he wanted an answer sooner. Would you mind taking a look at the wall space and deciding? We discussed the showing more times than I can count. I'm sure you can be as much help to him as I would be."

"You'd trust me to do that?" she said, overwhelmed by his easy confidence in her.

"Yes, without question." His voice was deeper, darker.

"I'll call Tom tomorrow. I can't wait to see you," she said softly.

"Same here. What are you wearing?"

The switch of subject caught her off guard and she looked blankly down at her pajamas. "A white cotton tank top and blue sleep shorts. Why?"

"I was hoping you were naked," he told her. "But I can picture you in pajamas, too. Cute, right?"

She laughed. "Well, the pajamas are cute—that's why I bought them."

"Then you are, too," he said with satisfaction. "And sexy."

"They aren't exactly the same as lacy black lingerie, Eli," she said dryly.

"Honey, on you, everything's sexy."

His voice made her shiver and sent heat rolling through her veins, tightening her nerves with anticipation.

"Stop that," she murmured, her own voice throaty. "You're too far away for me to seduce."

He sighed. "Sorry, honey. I promise we'll take care of that the minute I get to New York."

Amanda would be counting the minutes.

But just over a week later, Eli's plane was late and plans had been changed. Getting Amanda alone for some much needed one-on-one time would have to wait. Her family had insisted on welcoming him to New York with dinner.

Eli had time only to drop his suitcase in his hotel room, quickly shower and change clothes before catching a taxi to the restaurant.

He'd adjusted to the quietness of rural life over the past month. There, the cry of a hawk high overhead, a bugling call from Jiggs or the chug of the tractor were the loudest noises he heard. Here in the city, sound was a backdrop for the throngs of people on the sidewalks and the traffic clogging the streets. The loud thump-thump of bass pounding out of speakers grew louder before fading away as a battered car driven by a twentysomething guy pulled even with the cab and then turned at the end of the block. Up front, the cabbie's radio squawked with intermittent static.

The city hummed with all the human activity that was absent on the Triple C. Eli sat back and enjoyed the quick snapshots of the city outside the cab's windows.

The restaurant where Amanda had chosen to gather the family to meet him was Italian, and as he stepped inside, the smells of red sauce and sausage, rich cheese and good wine assaulted his senses. He scanned the room, searching for Amanda. He found her just as she stood, leaving the group surrounding a table near the back to walk toward him, a smile of welcome lighting her face.

"Hi," he told her. With unselfconscious ease, she hugged him, going up on tiptoe to brush a kiss against his cheek before catching his hand in hers. He fought the urge to pull her into his arms and kiss her properly and won, but just barely.

"Hi," she replied. "I'm so glad you're finally here. Come meet everyone."

Her fingers threaded through his, she drew him with her as they wound their way around other diners to reach the table set for seven.

"Eli, this is my mom and dad, Connie and George, and my sister, Lindsey, and her husband, Tom. The little one chewing her binky is Emma. Everyone, this is Eli," Amanda said, beaming at him.

There was a round of hellos. Eli shook George's and Tom's hands before seating Amanda and slipping into the remaining vacant chair.

"We've ordered family style," Amanda told him. "We come here often and the owner always has a wonderful variety and includes salad and bread."

"Sounds good," Eli told her.

"Are you hungry? What did they feed you on the plane?" she asked.

"I'm starved," he said with feeling. "The flight meal was a sandwich and chips."

"I hope you're ready to greet a crowd at the gallery," Tom said from across the table. "The auction is only five days away and the buzz about the exhibition unveiling your mother's work is getting frantic."

"I'm hoping that translates into a lot of bidding," Eli responded.

Tom grinned. "I think that's a given," he said with complete confidence. "Just the fact that new Melanie Coulter work is on the market will pull in serious collectors, but twenty-two sculptures, previously unseen, well…" He paused significantly. "The gallery has had so many inquiries about the pieces that we had to assign an assistant to deal with callers nearly full-time."

"That's good news," Eli said with feeling. "Let's just hope they bring their wallets with them to the auction."

Tom laughed. "The collectors I've spoken with are very interested and they have deep pockets."

"Good." Eli felt a deep twist of satisfaction. He wouldn't count on anything until the auction itself was over, but Tom's comments made hope move higher. Maybe they could save the ranch, after all.

"I wanted to thank you for being so hospitable to Amanda while she was visiting Montana, Eli," Amanda's mother put in from down the table, leaning forward to smile at him.

"It was my pleasure, Mrs. Blake," Eli told her politely.

Beneath the cover of the white tablecloth, Amanda's fingers threaded through his, their hands palm to palm. The pressure of her hand squeezing his made promises for later.

By the time they reached Amanda's apartment later that evening, both were long past being patient. Eli pulled her into his arms the moment the door closed behind them and they kissed feverishly, shedding clothes and laughing as she tugged him down the hall to her bedroom.

They made love and held each other until nearly dawn.

It wasn't until he was nearly asleep that Eli realized he hadn't told her about the engagement ring in his coat pocket.

Tomorrow, he thought hazily just before sleep claimed him. *I'll ask her to marry me tomorrow.*

But somehow, in the rush of busy, happy days, he kept putting off asking Amanda if she'd marry him and return to Montana.

The days flew by. Amanda and Eli were nearly insep-arable as she took him on tours of her favorite neighbor-hoods, her favorite coffee shop. They walked through Central Park, sitting on a bench to eat hot dogs and watch children playing on the grass.

Eli had visited New York City before but now he saw it through Amanda's eyes. For her, this was home. She'd been born and raised here, her close-knit family all lived here and she clearly loved it.

As the hours and days slipped away, he became more and more convinced that he couldn't ask Amanda to give up her life here in New York to marry him and live in Montana.

There were many things about the city that Eli liked, too, but if he couldn't ask Amanda to leave New York, he was forced to consider whether he could leave Mon-tana and live here full-time.

And the answer was no.

Somewhere between leaving Spain and now, his roots had sunk deep into Triple C's acres once more. He didn't want to, couldn't, rip them up again.

The engagement ring he'd taken from the studio vault, the one created by his mother that matched the ones he'd given to Cade and Zach for their future brides, remained in his pocket. He never removed it, but nei-ther did he tell Amanda he carried it.

If he'd loved her less, maybe he would have proposed and seduced her into returning to the Triple C with him. But he couldn't do that to her. Even if she agreed, how long would it be before she was miserable away from her family, friends and the life she loved?

When the auction was over, he'd fly back to Montana, alone.

In the meantime, he cherished each moment with Amanda, though the time was bittersweet.

The auction of Melanie Coulter's sculptures was a smashing success. Even Eli hadn't expected the crowd of collectors that mobbed the gallery. When the evening was over, the doors locked behind the last guest, and Tom told him the total dollar amount they'd made from the sales, Eli was dumbstruck.

He could easily pay his share of the tax debt on the Triple C.

Tom opened a bottle of champagne and Eli, Amanda and Lindsey joined him in toasting their success.

It was after 2:00 a.m. when Amanda and Eli returned to Eli's hotel, leaving the taxi to walk the last block.

"I love New York." Amanda smiled, looking up at the flashing neon sign on the top of the tall building. Arms held out, she twirled in a circle, laughing. "I've missed it."

Eli laughed, catching her hand when one of her stiletto heels caught on a crack in the sidewalk and she would have stumbled. "Careful, honey. You don't want to fall and break something."

"You'd catch me," she said with certainty. "Will you always catch me, Eli?"

"Absolutely," he said without pause. "But you might want to cut back on the champagne if I'm not around, just in case you feel like spinning in circles on sidewalks."

She wrapped her arms around his neck, her laughter effortlessly charming him.

"Let's go to your room," she murmured against his mouth.

Eli kissed her, heat simmering between them, before he raised his head, tucked her under his arm, and took her into his hotel, up the elevator and into his room.

They made love with an intensity that shook him. And when she finally fell asleep in his arms, Eli remained awake. Unwilling to give up a moment of these last hours with her to sleep, he stared at the ceiling and wondered how the hell he was going to survive without her.

Amanda woke slowly the next morning. Eyes closed, she rolled over, her hand searching for Eli. But the bed was empty. She opened her eyes and sat up, clutching the sheet. She was naked beneath it, and she took it with her as she slipped off the bed, wrapping it around her like a sarong.

A room service tray sat on the small table near the window and she poured herself coffee, sipping as she crossed to the bathroom. The door was open, the room steamy, and Eli stood in front of the counter, packing his shaving gear into his leather kit.

"Good morning," she said, smiling when he turned to her, his eyes heating as he took in her naked shoulders and the slipping sheet. She grasped the upper edge with one hand.

"Good morning." He leaned in and kissed her, his arm slipping around her waist to pull her close when the kiss turned hotter.

When he let her go, she was breathless.

"What a lovely way to say good morning," she said, her voice husky.

He smiled at her. "Don't spill your coffee." He nudged her hand with his, leveling the tilting cup.

She followed him out of the bathroom and realized his suitcase was open on the rack, the hangers above empty because he'd already folded his shirts and slacks into the case.

"You're packing?"

"Yes." He looked up at her, then bent to stow the leather bag with his shaving gear in the suitcase. "I have to catch a flight this morning."

"You're leaving *today*?" She stared at him. "You didn't tell me."

"No." His voice was gentle. "Like you, I hate saying goodbyes."

"I thought you might stay a few days. We haven't been to the Statue of Liberty yet. And we talked about driving upstate, out in the country...." Her voice trailed off.

"I need to get home, Amanda. Now that Mom's collection is sold, my brothers and I have to talk to the tax people, work out a plan for paying off the last of the inheritance tax on the ranch."

"Of course." She was reeling, knocked off balance at the realization that he must have planned all along to leave today. While they'd been making love last night, he'd known, she thought. He'd known he was leaving this morning. She felt like she was bleeding inside. "When will I see you again?"

"Tom wants me to put together a collection for his gallery, so I'll be back in New York for the opening sometime during the next few months or so. And if you're in Montana, you're always welcome at the Triple C."

"I see, of course." She could hardly force her throat open to breathe, let alone speak.

He closed the zipper on the suitcase and set it near the door, took his jacket from the back of the chair.

"Amanda…" He moved closer, lifted his hand as if to touch her face.

She shifted back, putting space between them, knowing that if he touched her, she'd break apart.

"Why are you doing this, Eli?" She struggled not to cry.

"You belong here in New York, Amanda. And I belong in Montana. Too many miles separate us—visits are all we can have."

"Really?" Anger rose, hot and consuming. "So we'll…what? See each other whenever we happen to be in the same town? Have great reunion sex every now and then?"

He winced, his mouth flattening. "That's not what I meant, Amanda…"

"You'd better go. You don't want to miss your plane."

He stared at her, green eyes roiling with emotion, a muscle flexing along the grim set of his jawline.

"Yeah, I'd better go," he said at last.

He stared at her, as if willing her to speak, but she tilted her chin up and stared at him without blinking, unwilling to lay her heart open when he was clearly ready to walk away.

He bit off a curse and pulled the door open, caught the handle of his suitcase and stepped into the hall.

And he was gone.

Amanda stared at the blank white door, unmoving,

until she was sure there was no chance he was coming back. Then she crumpled to the floor, harsh sobs racking her body with grief, heartbreak and shattered dreams.

Chapter Twelve

Three weeks later the phone rang in her quiet apartment, startling Amanda. She left her computer and padded across the living room carpet to reach it. Her breath caught when she recognized the Montana area code.

"Hello?" *It has to be Eli,* she thought, her heart pounding with adrenaline and conflicted emotion. *Who else would call me from Montana?*

"Hi, Amanda. This is Mariah."

Her heart plummeted. The rapid descent from emotional high to disappointing low was disorienting.

"Hello, Mariah," she managed to get out. "How nice to hear from you. How are you?"

"Fine, just fine. I'm at the Lodge and Cynthia is here, too. She says hello."

Amanda smiled. "Tell her hello for me—and tell her I miss having lunch with you two and Jane. I especially miss Jane's cooking."

Mariah laughed. "I'll tell them. How's the book coming along?"

They chatted for several moments, catching up on the big and small details of their lives, before Mariah's voice was suddenly more solemn.

"Listen, I know it's none of my business, Amanda, and feel free to tell me to butt out, but…did you and Eli have a fight while he was in New York for the auction?"

Startled, Amanda frowned in confusion. "No. Why? Did he say we had an argument?"

"He's not saying anything," Mariah said. "That's the problem."

"I'm afraid I don't understand."

"Eli's been in the world's worst mood ever since he came home from New York," Mariah told her. "None of us can figure out why, especially since the auction went so well. In fact, it exceeded everyone's wildest expectations," she added. "Which is why we're all confused as to why he's so grouchy. He acts like he's lost his best friend."

Good, Amanda thought. *At least I'm not the only one who's miserable.* "I thought he seemed happy enough while he was here," she said aloud.

Which isn't a lie, she told herself. *I thought we were falling in love. Right up until he said goodbye and I realized I was the only one who'd fallen.*

"So, nothing significant happened?" Mariah asked.

"I'm not aware of anything, but maybe he had a problem of some sort with the gallery. I could ask my brother-in-law, if you'd like me to—he owns the gallery that handled the auction."

"No, thanks." Mariah sighed, clearly confused and

still worried. "I just thought…well, after Cade told me Eli took one of Melanie's rings with him to New York, I assumed…"

Amanda frowned, certain she'd misunderstood. "Eli had one of his mother's rings with him? One of the rings from her collection? The group that you and Cynthia received engagement rings from?"

"Yes, yes and yes," Mariah replied. "I thought maybe he'd proposed and you turned him down. That would certainly explain his foul mood since he came home. But if he didn't propose, then there goes my theory."

"He didn't propose." Amanda blinked back sudden tears. "And from conversations I had with him while in Montana, I'm convinced there's little chance he ever would, Mariah."

"I'm sorry to hear that." Mariah's voice was softly sympathetic. "I thought you were good for Eli. You made him relax, made him laugh."

"Yes, well, I doubt Eli would agree." Amanda ran her fingertips over her eyelashes, wiping away dampness, and cleared her throat, which seemed clogged with unshed tears. "How's Brodie doing? Has he signed up for physical therapy yet?"

Mariah accepted the clear signal that Amanda didn't want to discuss Eli any longer. The two chatted for a few more moments about acquaintances in Indian Springs before saying goodbye.

Amanda returned the portable phone to its base, staring unseeingly at the family photos that hung on the wall, before she shook her head to clear it and turned away.

Mariah must have been wrong about Eli taking an engagement ring to New York.

Grieving over Eli Coulter was unproductive, she told herself firmly. Besides, it wasn't his fault that he didn't love her back. A person couldn't choose who they loved and who they didn't. Ending up with a broken heart was her own fault, the result of ignoring her normal caution and jumping recklessly into a heated affair while hoping it would all work out.

Somehow, knowing she'd set herself up for a broken heart and only had herself to blame didn't make her feel any better.

Eli stared at the television set. The sound of crowds cheering as one of the teams on the screen scored grew louder, then faded away. He hardly noticed.

"You know, since you came home from New York, you've been partying too much."

Eli blinked, turned his head to look at Brodie, stretched out in the recliner, and struggled to process his brother's words.

"What are you talking about? I've barely been off the ranch since I got back," he replied, frowning in confusion.

"Yeah," Brodie drawled. "That's my point. What's going on with you? 'Cause you're sure as hell not acting normal."

Eli stiffened. "I'm normal," he growled.

"Right." Brodie smirked. "What happened to the cute little girl from New York? I thought you might be bringing her home with you."

"You thought wrong." Eli bit off the words.

"Did she turn you down?" Brodie asked mildly.

Eli wished he'd stop asking questions. "Did she turn down what?"

"When you asked her to marry you and come back to the Triple C," Brodie said with more patience than he usually displayed. "Did she say no?"

"I didn't ask her."

"Well, that's a bonehead move," Brodie said with typical bluntness. "I liked her. You seemed good with her, like the two of you fit."

"Yeah, well, we didn't." Eli stared broodingly at the screen without seeing the game.

"What happened?"

"Nothing happened," Eli said shortly. "I flew to New York for the auction, we had a few laughs and I came home. End of story."

"Huh," Brodie grunted.

When he didn't say more, Eli looked at him. The sympathy in his brother's green eyes made him feel worse.

"What?" he demanded.

"You've got woman trouble and you're too stubborn to admit it," Brodie told him.

"I don't have woman trouble," Eli said, irritated. "Her life is in New York. Mine is here on the ranch. What I've got is a woman who belongs in her world and it's halfway across the country."

"So go get her and bring her out here. Then you'll both be in the same place. End of problem," Brodie said reasonably.

"No, not the end of the problem. That's the beginning of the problem," Eli said morosely.

"I don't follow your reasoning."

Eli pushed to his feet and paced across the room, then back. "What kind of a person would I be if I seduced her into leaving her home and her friends, where she's happy and loves her life, to come live with me? Sure, I'd have her here, but she'd have to leave everything she loves." He shoved his hands into the back pockets of his jeans and paced across the living room again. "And if I moved to New York to be with her, how long would it be before I grew to hate the city? How long before we started fighting because one of us was miserable and homesick and blaming the other for it?" He shook his head, dropping back onto the sofa, his face morose.

"You make it sound like it's either/or, with no middle ground," Brodie said mildly. "Why don't you split your time between the Triple C and New York? Not that I'm crazy about the idea of your being gone half the time, but hell, having you here when you're this miserable without her isn't exactly happy times."

Eli glared at him. "You think I haven't thought about that?" He shook his head. "It wouldn't work. She has a job in New York and she's damn good at it."

"I thought she was writing a book," Brodie said. "Can't she do that anywhere?"

"She took a six-month leave from her job to write the book about Mom," Eli told him. "Her regular job is at an art magazine with offices in New York."

"And she told you she wants to go back to work there when the book is finished?" Brodie asked.

"We didn't talk about it," Eli said.

"Well, that doesn't make any sense. Don't you think you should ask her and find out if she does?" Brodie's voice had a pronounced "duh" inflection.

Eli glared at him. "Lucky you're not in any shape for a brawl, or I'd punch you for that," he said.

Brodie grinned. "I could still take you out, kid, with one hand tied behind my back and my leg in a cast."

"Big talk." A reluctant grin curved Eli's mouth. He sat forward, elbows propped on his knees, and ran his hands through his hair. "Straight up, Brodie, I'm miserable without her."

"Then go get her." Brodie's voice was gentler, matter-of-fact. "I don't claim to know much about women. You probably should be having this talk with Cade or Zach, but one thing I do know is life's too short to waste time." He tapped his thigh. "A year ago I was riding high. Now I have no idea what the hell I'm going to do with the rest of my life. If you care about her, go get her."

"She might refuse to talk to me," Eli admitted.

Brodie shrugged. "Maybe she will. Maybe she won't. Do you want to keep moping around the ranch, making yourself and everyone else miserable?"

"Is that what I'm doing?"

"Yeah, pretty much," Brodie answered.

"Well, hell, we can't have that." Eli stood and headed for the stairs.

"Where are you going?" Brodie called after him.

"Upstairs to pack my bag. I've got a plane to catch."

"About damn time," Brodie growled, the grin on his face belying the rough rumble of his voice.

A day later Amanda's doorbell rang just after 10:00 p.m.

"What on earth?" she muttered, glancing at the clock. She wasn't expecting company. In fact, she'd showered and donned pajamas an hour earlier, settling in with a bowl of popcorn and a movie on DVD. The popcorn bowl was now empty and the movie two-thirds finished.

She thumbed the Pause button on the remote control, tossed it on the sofa cushion and crossed the room to the door.

She peered through the tiny surveillance glass and gasped. Her caller was tall, black-haired, and stood with one hand shoved in his slacks pocket, a jacket slung over his other shoulder.

As she watched, she saw him shake hands with her neighbor and realized Mrs. Ferguson must have brought him up with her after walking her dog. The widow had met Eli when he was in town for the gallery showing and had been completely charmed by the handsome artist.

But what was Eli doing in New York—in her hallway?

He rang the bell again. She cast a frantic glance in the small mirror next to the door, smoothed a hand over her hair, groaned at the lack of makeup, and forced herself to draw a deep breath and slowly release it. Then she pulled open the door.

"Eli, what a surprise. Come in." She held the door open wide and he stepped inside, half turning to look down at her as she pushed the door shut and slid the dead bolt home. "What are you doing in New York?"

She looked up at him, hoping her face didn't reflect the almost painful surge of joy that swept her as she took in the angles of his face, the pale lake-water green of his eyes, the way his thick lashes half lowered as he looked at her.

Dear God, she'd missed him. It made her heart hurt just to look at him.

"Amanda…" His deep voice broke off and he dropped his jacket, reaching for her.

His hands caught her waist, finding the bare skin between the hem of her short cotton tee and the waistband of her sleep shorts, and he pulled her forward.

She lifted on her toes as his head bent and their mouths met in a kiss that burned away any pretense that this was casual. Amanda clung to him and he pressed her closer, tighter against his hard body. He was all hard angles and planes, and her softer curves molded against him. Aroused male against heated female. She couldn't get close enough and she groaned her approval when he backed her against the door, his big body covering hers.

His mouth was ravenous; his hand smoothed over her hip, thigh, stroking up over her belly to cup her breast. Her hands clenched, fingers tightening, and she slid the bare sole of her foot up the outside of his leg in an effort to get closer.

She heard him groan, felt the fierce grip of his hands as he tensed before he raised his head.

"We have to talk before we do this, Amanda." His voice rasped, his chest rising and falling rapidly.

"You want to *talk?*" She struggled to understand.

"I just have to ask you a couple of questions...." He groaned when she shifted to fit her hips more tightly against his. "No, baby, please, don't move."

She stilled, staring up at him. The planes of his face were flushed; his cheekbones dark with color; his eyes fierce with arousal.

"First, I just wanted to say I'm sorry. I'm sorry for being such a jerk and running off like a coward. I have no excuse. The bottom line is, I just got scared. I've never been in love before and the idea of it scared the pants off me."

Amanda was convinced she was hearing things. "Wait a minute. What did you just say?"

"I love you, Amanda Blake. Can you ever forgive me for being such a fool?"

Amanda's vision blurred with tears. She laid her palms against his cheeks. "Yes," she whispered. "Oh, yes. I love you, too. So much."

His eyes closed, his forehead resting against hers as he drew in a deep, harsh breath. "Thank God." He kissed her tenderly.

Amanda realized what it had cost him to come here and bare his soul to her. It confirmed what she'd sensed between them from the start. But it left her with more questions than answers.

"So," she began. "Where do we go from here?"

Eli sighed. "I'm not sure. All I know is that I'm miserable without you. Shakira misses you too. Would you…would you consider coming back to the Triple C? At least until Christmas?"

Amanda understood that Eli wasn't ready to make a long-term commitment. She wasn't sure if she was, either. The one thing she was sure of, though, was that she was not ready to let him go.

"Christmas at the Triple C. That sounds perfect," she said.

Eli shook his head. "You may change your mind after you've experienced winter on a ranch. That can be tough for even native Montana folks."

Amanda smile gamely. "At least we'll have our love to keep us warm."

"I don't deserve you, but I'll try my best to make you happy, I swear I will." The solemn words in his deep voice were a vow.

She smiled, tasting the salt of tears at the corner of her mouth. "I know you will," she murmured. If she still harbored any doubts, she was willing to table them… at least for now.

His lips brushed over her face in small, reverent kisses, replacing the tears, until his mouth sealed over hers.

Long heated moments later he raised his head and looked down at her. She knew what he was asking.

He swung her into his arms and carried her toward her bedroom. They might not know exactly what would happen next, but Amanda felt they were finally heading in the right direction.

Chapter Thirteen

The first snowflakes didn't start to fall until early November. Amanda woke early one morning knowing something was different but unable to pinpoint exactly what it was.

She lay snug and warm in the big new bed Eli had moved into his bedroom. Beneath a bright blue Pendleton wool blanket and crisp white sheets, she was curled on her side with her body tucked against the warm, hard length of Eli's. His arm was a welcome weight at her waist, anchoring her against him, his hair-roughened thighs pressed against the back of hers.

Amanda smiled and pressed a little closer to the hard male warmth. Eli muttered unintelligibly and hauled her closer without waking.

It was all she could do not to laugh out loud. He was incredibly possessive, even while asleep, she thought.

As she lay there, held safe in his arms, a deep sense

of contentment warmed her from the inside out. She understood Eli's concerns that she have a chance to know what life here on the Triple C could be like in winter. She imagined the challenge of enduring potentially isolating snowstorms.

But after sharing the past weeks since they'd returned from New York, she'd become more convinced daily that she could live in the Arctic if Eli was there. Not that anyone had invited her to stay.

The muted sounds of movement downstairs told her Brodie was awake and heading for the kitchen.

Amanda carefully lifted Eli's arm from around her waist and slipped out of bed. She grabbed her fleece robe from the chair and slipped into it, bending to press a light kiss against Eli's beard-roughened cheek before walking to the window.

She caught her breath, her eyes widening with delight. Outside, snowflakes drifted lazily to the earth. The buildings and grounds were lightly frosted with white, the fence posts and gate directly below the window boasting little caps of snow.

"Eli, wake up." She spun and hurried back to the bed, bending to catch his hand in hers.

"What?" His deep voice was rough with sleep; his eyes heavy-lidded beneath tousled black hair.

"Snow! It's snowing outside."

"Is that all?" He chuckled, his smile indulgent. "I told you it would be, sooner or later."

"I know you did, but 'sooner or later' isn't the same as now." She tugged on his hand. "Come see."

He tossed back the blankets and let her pull him from the bed to the window. He wrapped his arms around her waist, enfolding her, her weight resting against him as they looked out the window.

The snowflakes continued to drift earthward, their number increasing to deepen the layer of fluffy white icing on the ground, roofs and fence posts.

"It really is beautiful," Amanda said, tilting her head back to look up at Eli, her loose hair sliding against the heavy muscles of his bare chest.

"The first snow of the season always is," he agreed. He looked down at her. "I hope you still feel that way by December."

"I will," she said firmly.

He brushed a kiss against her lips. "I'm counting on it," he murmured. "How about we get dressed, grab some coffee and go outside?"

She smiled up at him, anticipation spiking. "Can we take the dogs and go for a walk?"

"If you want to." He bent and kissed her, his arms tightening, molding her against him as the kiss deepened, turned hotter.

When Eli tugged the tie loose and her robe parted, letting their bodies press skin to skin, Amanda didn't protest.

They didn't make it downstairs for another hour.

"Good morning," Brodie greeted them from the living room.

"Morning," Eli replied, pausing with Amanda on their way to the kitchen. "Did you have breakfast already?"

Brodie nodded. "Eggs and bacon. I left a plate with extra crispy on the counter."

"Yum, perfect. Can we get you anything?" Amanda asked. "Coffee?"

He lifted his mug. "Just refilled it." He gave her a faint grin when she smiled at him.

Amanda entered the kitchen behind Eli. "How do you think he's doing?" she asked, crossing to join Eli at the coffeemaker.

"What do you mean?" he asked, handing her a steaming mug before picking up his own.

"Do you think he's healing well?" Amanda frowned, faint worry niggling at her.

"He says he's a million times better than he was in the summer." Eli too, frowned slightly. "But when he thinks no one is looking, he looks like he's hurting."

"Is there anything we can do?" Amanda had grown fond of Eli's brother over the past weeks. After observing him with Jane's little boy, and the puppies, and experiencing his kindness herself, she'd decided that the dark, often moody Brodie had a softer, gentler side.

Eli raked his fingers through his hair, clearly concerned. "I don't know what it would be. But if you think of anything, let me know." He cupped her cheek in the palm of one big hand, his thumb stroking her bottom lip. "I appreciate your being okay with us staying here in the house with him."

"I wouldn't have it any other way," she assured him. "He's family and I know how worried you've been." She covered his hand with her own, trapping his fingers against her cheek. "I think it's wonderful that you and your brothers care so much for him. And besides," she added with a smile, "he makes killer breakfasts."

"Yeah, he does that." Eli pressed a slow, sweet kiss against her mouth.

Her coffee forgotten, Amanda welcomed the wave of love, lust and emotion that took her under.

He raised his head, his warm breath ghosting over her kiss-dampened lips. "I love you."

Her vision instantly misted. "I love you, too," she murmured back.

"Breakfast," Eli declared, releasing her with obvious reluctance. "Or we'll end up back upstairs in bed and you won't get to go walking in the snow."

They left the house not quite an hour later. Amanda wore a thigh-length jacket over her jeans with knee-high UGG boots and wool gloves that matched her white knit hat and muffler. Eli's only concession to the cold was a sheepskin-lined coat and gloves. He replaced his usual cowboy boots with pac boots, but unlike Amanda, he opted for his black Stetson instead of a knit hat.

The air was crisp and clean; the silence unbroken.

"I love this!" Amanda exclaimed, turning in a circle with her arms outstretched. "Let's get the puppies and take them with us."

Eli grinned indulgently and caught her hand in his as they crossed the pristine, unmarked white expanse of the ranch yard to reach the barn. When they stepped inside, they were greeted with the whicker of Jiggs and Shakira, still in their box stalls. A chorus of sharp barks filled the air as the rottweiler pups added their voices to the horses'.

"Jeez, you guys are noisy." Eli entered Shakira's stall, Amanda following him. While he checked the water level in Shakira's bucket, she petted the pretty mare.

Then Eli unlatched and swung wide the outer door to the corral and Shakira exited, pausing just outside to lower her head and sniff the snow.

"Let's let Jiggs out," Eli said.

Moments later he pushed open the stall door and the

black stallion quickly moved into the corral. He joined
Shakira in nosing the snow, pawing experimentally;
then the two of them raced around the corral fence.

"I think they like it," Amanda observed, laughing
when the two horses bucked and kicked, looking for all
the world like two children racing and playing.

She looked up at Eli, standing beside her in the open
doorway, and noted the quirk of his lips as he watched
the horses play.

"I think you're right," he said.

Behind them, the dogs barked louder.

"Dogs next," Eli said, turning Amanda back into the
barn. She crossed the aisle while he closed the door, and
he joined her as she reached the stall where the pups
were contained. Black muzzles poked through the open
sections between the slats while other pups leapt in a
frenzied attempt to join them.

"Hi there," Amanda crooned, laughing when Eli
opened the gate and the eight puppies spilled out in a
mad tumble of wriggling, overjoyed furry bodies. Their
mother ambled out more slowly, pausing to receive a
pat.

"Watch out." Eli wrapped his arm around Amanda's
waist to keep her from being bowled over. "Are you
sure you want to take them with us?" he said dryly as
they were surrounded by bouncing, jumping half-grown
dogs.

"Absolutely."

They left the barn, the pups racing ahead of them
and out the half-open door. By the time Eli and Amanda
stepped outside, the dogs were rolling in the snow, then
standing to shake the cold white stuff off their fur.

"They're hilarious," Amanda commented as Eli took

her hand and they headed down the lane past the barn and toward the studio and Lodge.

"They're crazy," Eli said bluntly, but he laughed out loud when two of the dogs grabbed the same stick and tugged, their faces comical with surprise when their feet slid out from under them and they sprawled in the snow.

"But they're fun," Amanda said. "Is Cade going to keep them all?"

"He said several neighbors have approached him about adopting some of them, but to be honest, I think my brother is having trouble giving them up."

"I hope he asks Brodie and Jane's little boy before picking any of them to give away," Amanda said. "They're both really attached to the dogs."

"Yeah, they are." Eli grew thoughtful. "And what about you?"

"I'm a little attached," she admitted. But she knew better than to say any more. She and Eli never talked about the future. He was a bit like a skittish horse, and she was afraid that too much pressure might send him running.

Eli pulled her to a stop, his hands at her waist as he eased her closer, until her thighs rested against his and her hands lifted to clasp the heavy jacket over his biceps.

"What?" she asked when he stared intently down at her for a long, silent moment.

"You're an amazing woman, Amanda Blake," he murmured.

He bent his head, his lips warm against hers, chasing away the chill of the frosty morning. As always when he kissed her, Amanda felt the world slip away.

The sounds of the dogs barking and gamboling around them grew muted, the world narrowing to Eli's heat and his arms around her.

Long moments passed before they moved on, their boots kicking up snow as they continued down the lane. They passed the studio with its roof and deck frosted in white and kept walking. Only the creak of tree limbs as they bent under the growing weight of snow and the yips and barks of the pups broke the silence.

"Mariah is excited about all of you being home for Christmas," Amanda commented. "She wants to have everyone stay in rooms at the Lodge for a few days so we're all together for one long celebration. Cade told her your mother started that tradition."

"Yeah, Mom loved decorating the Lodge for the holidays." Eli's gaze grew slightly unfocused, as if he was seeing memories. "We'd wake up on Christmas morning and race down to the lobby, where Dad always had a fire going in the fireplace. Piles of presents were under the tree and our stockings were stuffed with gifts and hanging from the mantel."

"It sounds lovely," Amanda said, tucking her hand through the crook of his arm. Beside, ahead and behind them, the half-grown rottweiler puppies romped and played, tunneling their noses through the snow until they had little piles of cold white stacked on top of their muzzles. They gamboled around Eli and Amanda, their glossy black-and-tan coats gleaming against the pristine white of the new coat of snow.

"We didn't celebrate Christmas after Mom was gone," Eli said idly, his gaze on the dogs. "I haven't thought about it much, but it might be nice to have all of us at the Lodge for Christmas Day again."

Amanda's heart caught. Each time Eli made an off-hand comment about his childhood in the years after his mother died, she wanted to hold him close and shelter the little boy he'd once been. But the man was always so matter-of-fact about what sounded to her like emotionally barren years that she always forced herself not to overreact. She knew that the loss of his mother—and those hard years afterward—were a large part of why Eli was so wary of commitment.

"I love the idea of having a family celebration at the Lodge," she said lightly. "And just FYI, Mr. Coulter, I love Christmas. So be prepared for major decorating and massive amounts of good food, including roast turkey and homemade fudge. And cookies. You'll have to help decorate cookies."

His face registered disbelief. "I have to decorate cookies? Can't I just eat them? You know, to make sure you baked correctly?"

"Nope, not nearly enough participation." She laughed when he groaned.

As Amanda contemplated the Christmas they would spend together, emotion slowly flooded her. She realized with a start that this was what it felt like to be completely content and happy. Even if their relationship was fated to end, she would cherish these weeks for the rest of her life.

The days rolled by. Busy and productive, Amanda was shocked to realize one morning that it was only two weeks until Christmas. Each day, she spent several hours working on the biography of Eli's mother and was happy with the results. When she sent her agent a preliminary draft, he responded with enthusiasm.

She reveled in the time she spent outdoors with Eli. Far from disliking the cold, snow and relative isolation on the Triple C, she found she loved the small community.

When Eli pulled her away from her computer one morning, insisting she had to come outside because he had a surprise for her, she donned her coat and went willingly.

He opened the door and she closed her eyes, letting him lead her out onto the porch.

"Can I open my eyes now?" she asked, one hand gripping Eli's wrist. Both of his hands were cupped over her eyes as he stood behind her, keeping her blindfolded. "Do I hear bells?" she added, tilting her head slightly to better define the jingling sound.

"Yes, you hear bells," Eli said with amusement. Then his hands lowered to rest on her shoulders.

Amanda's eyes popped open and she blinked, focusing.

"Oh, my," she said with awed delight. "It's gorgeous."

Just outside the gate sat an old-fashioned sleigh. The two-passenger seat was upholstered in black leather with tucks and buttons, and the polished black lacquer of the body was decorated with gold-pinstriped scrolling. A bright red Pendleton blanket had been tossed on the seat and Mariah's deep bay gelding was hitched between the shafts. The sleigh's curved black runners were shiny with wax.

"You like it?" Eli asked.

"I love it." She spun to look up at him. "Where on earth did you get it?"

"It belonged to Mom and Dad. Brodie found it in the storage building and started restoring it last month."

Eli pointed at the sleigh. "I did the painting, but Brodie welded and restored the body. He did a great job, don't you think?"

"I think you're both amazing. It's absolutely beautiful."

"I'm glad you like it. Want to go for a ride?"

"Yes." Amanda caught his hand and tugged him off the porch and down the walkway to the sleigh.

She paused to pet Sarge for a moment before Eli helped her up onto the seat and stepped up after her.

"Cover up," he instructed, lifting the blanket to tuck it around her. "The air will feel colder when we start moving."

Satisfied she was comfortable, he lifted the reins, and they were off.

Amanda quickly discovered that the breeze created by Sarge's swift trot chilled her, and she snuggled against Eli's side beneath the blanket. They moved quickly down the lane, past the barn and toward the studio and Lodge.

As they glided across the ranch, she could feel his eyes on her. "Eli?" she asked. "What's the matter? You look a little...I don't know. Nervous, maybe?"

"Amanda, I have something to ask you."

Her heart caught, her breath catching too on a swift inhale as she studied his face.

He tugged her gently closer under the warm woolen blanket.

"Amanda Blake, I love you more than I ever thought it was possible to care for anyone. I can't imagine having to live the rest of my life without you. I hope I'm not wrong, but I think it's possible you're okay with living here on the Triple C. In fact, you might even like it.

So…" He paused, searching her face. "Will you marry me and put me out of my misery?"

She smiled, her eyes misty at his words. "Oh, Eli. Are you sure? Are you absolutely sure? I don't want you to do this just because you think it's what I want. We have time, you know. Plenty of time."

"Amanda, if you don't say yes, I'm going to lose my mind."

"Well, then, yes. Yes! A thousand times yes!"

When they returned to the barn an hour later, she was chilled to the bone but she didn't care. After unhitching Sarge and giving him oats and water, they returned to the house.

They'd barely shed their coats inside when Brodie left his room and walked toward them down the hallway.

"Brodie!" Amanda caught the big man in a joyful hug and kissed him exuberantly on the cheek.

"What's that for?" he asked when she stepped back, his confused gaze going from her to Eli and back.

"She likes the sleigh," Eli said with a grin.

"I *love* the sleigh," Amanda emphasized. "Thank you so much for restoring it and for letting us use it."

Brodie ran his palm over his head, rumpling his black hair. "The sleigh's just as much Eli's as mine and he did a lot of the work on it," he said gruffly, clearly uncomfortable with her praise and thanks.

"I've already told him thank you," she said.

"Yeah, she did," Eli drawled, his gaze heating as it met hers.

"Am I missing something?" Brodie asked. "Is there something else you're not telling me?"

Amanda smiled shyly at Eli. She wasn't ready to share their secret with the world just yet.

Amanda decided it was time to change the subject. "You know, I could use some hot chocolate. I need something to warm me up. All that cold air chilled me to the bone."

The remaining two weeks until the holidays raced by. Amanda went to Billings to go Christmas shopping with Cynthia, Mariah and Jane. She'd ordered a beautiful full-color art book online that had a section on the work of Lucan Montoya to give to Eli, but she wanted something more personal. Nothing seemed perfect but she finally settled on a pair of butter-soft black leather driving gloves lined with fur. He'd mentioned that he needed a thinner, more flexible pair so he could better feel and gauge the tension on the reins when he drove the sleigh.

She also found several CDs of Spanish flamenco music by a guitarist she knew he liked.

The closer the hours drew to Christmas Day, the more she had to fight the nearly overwhelming need to broadcast their engagement. They had decided to make the announcement on December 25, when everyone was together. Amanda felt she was about to burst.

Following traditions established by Melanie Coulter, everyone went to Christmas Eve church services in Indian Springs, returning to the Lodge in a caravan.

It was after midnight before the Lodge lobby slowly emptied as the couples headed upstairs. Brodie retired first, his steps on the stairs slow and methodical. Cade and Mariah soon followed; then Zach and Cynthia said good-night, leaving Eli and Amanda alone in front of the brightly lit tree.

The lamps glowed softly, the fire in the hearth adding its red-gold gleam to the colored lights twinkling on the decorated fir. A large evergreen wreath hung above the fireplace mantel, the glossy sheen of green needles and its large red ribbon bow adding color to the gray river rock of the chimney.

"It's getting late. We should go up, too," Amanda said softly. She turned, but before she could take a second step away from him, he caught her fingers in his.

His grip on her hand swung her back to face him.

Eli reached into his coat pocket and drew out a small blue velvet jewelers' box. "You remember my mother made just a few rings. Mariah has one, and so does Cynthia. I'd be honored if you'd wear one, too."

Amanda gasped and felt her eyes widen. The engagement ring had a large marquise-cut diamond, and there was a wedding band that matched perfectly, the exquisite stones sparkling in the light.

"Oh, Eli, they're beautiful."

"The engagement ring is from my mother's collection, but I made the wedding ring myself." He slipped the engagement ring free and tucked the small box back into his pocket. Then he lifted her hand and slid the ring onto her finger before bending his head and brushing a kiss against the ring and her skin.

"The ring is not nearly as beautiful as you are," he told her, his hands settling at her waist to hold her. He bent his head, nuzzling the curve of her neck where shoulder met throat. "When can we get married? Soon, right?"

She laughed, eyes half closed as his warm lips moved

enticingly against her throat. "It takes a while to plan a wedding, Eli."

He raised his head. "We could fly to Las Vegas and be married tomorrow."

She laughed. "Don't you think we should tell your brothers first? Besides, I've always wanted a real wedding. A traditional wedding with a beautiful dress, flowers, bridesmaids and my parents there."

"Then that's what you'll have," he said promptly. "Where do you want to have it? New York City?"

"No, I'd like to fly my family and friends out and hold it here, at the Lodge." She looked up at him. "Do you think Zach would let us use the Lodge?"

He tucked a strand of hair behind her ear, his fingers lingering to brush over her cheek with a gentleness that matched the tenderness in his eyes. "I think Zach would be a happy camper if you decide to have the wedding here."

"And you?" she asked. "Would you like to get married here on the ranch—maybe on Valentine's Day?"

"Honey," he said, his deep voice serious. "I'd be happy if you said you wanted to get married at the bottom of the ocean. Having the wedding here on the Triple C is just a bonus. As long as I you say 'I do,' I'm good."

She smiled and looped her arms around his neck, testing the soft silkiness of the hair at his nape with her fingertips. "I really do love you...so much."

"And thank God for that," he muttered before he took her mouth with his. As Amanda closed her eyes, swept away as always by the magic of his lips on hers, she could only echo the sentiment.

After Amanda had been thoroughly kissed, Eli finally pulled away from her. Then he hollered up the stairs with the news they'd been suppressing for weeks. As his brothers came racing back down the stairs to share in their happiness, Amanda realized there was no place in the world she'd rather be.

* * * * *

Look for Brodie Coulter's story,
the next book in Lois Faye Dyer's
BIG SKY BROTHERS *miniseries*
for Harlequin Special Edition!
Coming in 2012

HEART & HOME

Heartwarming romances where love can
happen right when you least expect it.

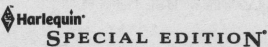
Harlequin
SPECIAL EDITION®

COMING NEXT MONTH
AVAILABLE NOVEMBER 22, 2011

#2155 TRUE BLUE
Diana Palmer

#2156 HER MONTANA CHRISTMAS GROOM
Montana Mavericks: The Texans Are Coming!
Teresa Southwick

#2157 ALMOST A CHRISTMAS BRIDE
Wives for Hire
Susan Crosby

#2158 A BABY UNDER THE TREE
Brighton Valley Babies
Judy Duarte

#2159 CHRISTMAS WITH THE MUSTANG MAN
Men of the West
Stella Bagwell

#2160 ROYAL HOLIDAY BRIDE
Reigning Men
Brenda Harlen

You can find more information on upcoming Harlequin® titles,
free excerpts and more at www.HarlequinInsideRomance.com.

HSECNM1111

REQUEST YOUR FREE BOOKS!
2 FREE NOVELS PLUS 2 FREE GIFTS!

SPECIAL EDITION
Life, Love & Family

YES! Please send me 2 FREE Harlequin® Special Edition novels and my 2 FREE gifts (gifts are worth about $10). After receiving them, if I don't wish to receive any more books, I can return the shipping statement marked "cancel." If I don't cancel, I will receive 6 brand-new novels every month and be billed just $4.49 per book in the U.S. or $5.24 per book in Canada. That's a saving of at least 14% off the cover price! It's quite a bargain! Shipping and handling is just 50¢ per book in the U.S. and 75¢ per book in Canada.* I understand that accepting the 2 free books and gifts places me under no obligation to buy anything. I can always return a shipment and cancel at any time. Even if I never buy another book, the two free books and gifts are mine to keep forever.

235/335 HDN FEGF

Name	(PLEASE PRINT)	
Address		Apt. #
City	State/Prov.	Zip/Postal Code

Signature (if under 18, a parent or guardian must sign)

Mail to the **Reader Service:**
IN U.S.A.: P.O. Box 1867, Buffalo, NY 14240-1867
IN CANADA: P.O. Box 609, Fort Erie, Ontario L2A 5X3

Not valid for current subscribers to Harlequin Special Edition books.

Want to try two free books from another line?
Call 1-800-873-8635 or visit www.ReaderService.com.

* Terms and prices subject to change without notice. Prices do not include applicable taxes. Sales tax applicable in N.Y. Canadian residents will be charged applicable taxes. Offer not valid in Quebec. This offer is limited to one order per household. All orders subject to credit approval. Credit or debit balances in a customer's account(s) may be offset by any other outstanding balance owed by or to the customer. Please allow 4 to 6 weeks for delivery. Offer available while quantities last.

Your Privacy—The Reader Service is committed to protecting your privacy. Our Privacy Policy is available online at www.ReaderService.com or upon request from the Reader Service.

We make a portion of our mailing list available to reputable third parties that offer products we believe may interest you. If you prefer that we not exchange your name with third parties, or if you wish to clarify or modify your communication preferences, please visit us at www.ReaderService.com/consumerschoice or write to us at Reader Service Preference Service, P.O. Box 9062, Buffalo, NY 14269. Include your complete name and address.

HSE11B

*Lucy Flemming and Ross Mitchell shared a magical,
sexy Christmas weekend together six years ago.
This Christmas, history may repeat itself when they find
themselves stranded in a major snowstorm...
and alone at last.*

Read on for a sneak peek from
IT HAPPENED ONE CHRISTMAS
by Leslie Kelly.

Available December 2011, only from Harlequin® Blaze™.

EYEING THE GRAY, THICK SKY through the expansive wall of
windows, Lucy began to pack up her photography gear.
The Christmas party was winding down, only a dozen or so
people remaining on this floor, which had been transformed
from cubicles and meeting rooms to a holiday funland. She
smiled at those nearest to her, then, seeing the glances at her
silly elf hat, she reached up to tug it off her head.

Before she could do it, however, she heard a voice. A
deep, male voice—smooth and sexy, and so not Santa's.

"I appreciate you filling in on such short notice. I've
heard you do a terrific job."

Lucy didn't turn around, letting her brain process what
she was hearing. Her whole body had stiffened, the hairs on
the back of her neck standing up, her skin tightening into
tiny goose bumps. Because that voice sounded so familiar.
Impossibly familiar.

It can't be.

"It sounds like the kids had a great time."

Unable to stop herself, Lucy began to turn around,
wondering if her ears—and all her other senses—were
deceiving her. After all, six years was a long time, the mind

could play tricks. What were the odds that she'd bump into *him,* here? And today of all days. December 23.

Six years exactly. Was that really possible?

One look—and the accompanying frantic thudding of her heart—and she knew her ears and brain were working just fine. Because it was *him.*

"Oh, my God," he whispered, shocked, frozen, staring as thoroughly as she was. "Lucy?"

She nodded slowly, not taking her eyes off him, wondering why the years had made him even more attractive than ever. It didn't seem fair. Not when she'd spent the past six years thinking he must have started losing that thick, golden-brown hair, or added a spare tire to that trim, muscular form.

No.

The man was gorgeous. Truly, without-a-doubt, mouthwateringly handsome, every bit as hot as he'd been the first time she'd laid eyes on him. She'd been twenty-two, he one year older.

They'd shared an amazing holiday season.

And had never seen one another again.

Until now.

Find out what happens in
IT HAPPENED ONE CHRISTMAS
by Leslie Kelly.
Available December 2011, only from Harlequin® Blaze™